I0533153

ON THE PROWL

TJ MICHAELS

ISBN-10: 0985787430
ISBN-13:978-0-9857874-3-1

DEDICATION

This book is dedicated to the two coolest people on earth, Tamara and Michael. For your understanding, inspiration and lots and lots of midnight tea runs, I appreciate you.

AUTHOR NOTE

Dear Reader,

This book, originally published as Primed to Pounce, was my debut novel. It was the first book to ever be contracted and published and was the beginning of my career as a professional author. It received a wonderful reception and great reviews. When the rights reverted from the publisher back to me, it was republished to ensure that you could still enjoy this particular world. So, here is On the Prowl in its entirety and original form. Enjoy!

With the greatest respect,

~TJ

CHAPTER ONE

"Thank you for flying US Airways. We'll land at Charlotte's Douglas Airport in approximately thirty minutes. Cabin crew, please prepare the cabin for landing."

All Delaine heard was "Yada, yada, yada, yada…" as she thought of her husband, well, her now ex-husband, for the trillionth time since he'd left her.

What the hell kind of man sends his wife an e-mail to tell her he's leaving her?

It's been a year and I still can't believe what he did, Delaine fumed inwardly, remembering that fateful morning as if it was yesterday. Her husband Gary had kissed her on his way out the door for work. Hell, he'd even told her to have a wonderful day. The last thing she'd expected when she arrived at her office was an e-mail from him giving her a two-day notice of his intentions to move out.

Delaine had been hurt and confused after reading his long rant of a jabbing e-mail. But when the light bulb in her head flipped on she'd been livid. No one simply blinked their eyes and had a whole new life, a new apartment and a new girlfriend without a little prep time. The bastard had planned his cowardly actions for weeks, maybe even months.

But unlike Gary, Delaine didn't have the option or desire to abandon her family. So she'd held it together, saw their twins off to college and was on her way to North Carolina on a new assignment for her agency.

She caught her reflection in the window. Dark brown, almond-shaped eyes twinkled intelligently in the dim overhead light. A slight smile graced her full, heart-shaped lips. She looked like a big kid in her baseball hat, leather bomber and jean shirt. Her cinnamon skin was flawless, and she couldn't see a single, easily identifiable wrinkle. In top physical shape and curvy in all the right places, at thirty-seven Delaine looked ten years younger. And her husband had left her because she had a habit of leaving her clothes on the bed? Shaking her head on a snort, she yanked her hat down over her brow and scooted down into the cushions of the leather chair. Well, at least she was headed to Charlotte first class.

She gazed out the small window at a beautiful pink and purple sunset, but all she saw was her hands wrapped firmly around Gary's neck as she squeezed. Hard. The image faded as Delaine's spirit guide whispered soothingly in her mind.

He is not worth the effort, Suta Winyan. He was not a worthy mate.

'I know, Sapa, I know,' Delaine sighed inwardly, sending the tired thoughts to the black mountain lion that shared her conscience.

The Great Spirit says this is meant to be. Good things are coming to you.

They landed without a hitch and Delaine was standing at baggage claim within fifteen minutes of deplaning. A loud siren blared, signaling the start of the conveyor belt just as a graying older gentleman, dressed in a classic black chauffeur jacket, white shirt and black trousers, approached. The sign he carried held her initials written in bold, black letters.

"Ms. D.J.?" he asked politely.

Delaine nodded with a friendly smile at the man's welcome attempt at discretion. After all, she was undercover. It wouldn't do to have her name plastered on a sign for all to see.

"My name is Timmons, and I'll be your driver tonight," he said, with a tip of his hat and a slight bow. "I'll retrieve your luggage and we'll be on our way shortly, ma'am."

Delaine waited patiently in the arriving passenger area while Timmons brought the car around—a white Crown Victoria limousine, courtesy of her company, Aegis Analytical. Her belongings were quickly stowed in the spacious trunk, and a very polite Timmons settled her into the spacious backseat. Without a word, he passed her a large sealed manila envelope, climbed into the driver's seat and they were off.

She flipped on the reading lamp and kicked off her shoes. The big backseat was perfect for sprawling, and Delaine mentally thanked her boss, Geri, for arranging a private car to take her to her new home.

Delaine allowed her tired body to sink into the plush leather cushions then carefully opened the flap on the envelope. It was stuffed with several items, some she would need immediately. She pulled out the keys to her new house and a note from her boss confirming the date of delivery of the rest of her belongings. Also the spare keys to her car, which she'd gone without for the past couple of weeks so it could be shipped ahead, and another note from the transport coordinator—the car was now parked in her driveway just waiting for her to arrive.

The envelope also contained the results of a few special strings Geri pulled in consideration of Delaine's unexpected status of single mom—a bank receipt for a hefty moving bonus, already deposited in a bank in Charlotte, and airline e-tickets for her children, who would fly to Charlotte for their Christmas break instead of Denver. Thanks to Geri, the exchange of the plane tickets hadn't cost a dime.

There was a second manila envelope buried in the bottom of the first. Delaine tucked it into the side pocket of her carry-on bag. She knew from experience that this one pertained to her mission. She'd wait until she was in the privacy of her home before she opened it.

Delaine flipped the reading light off, leaned her head back against the seat and peered out the window. It wasn't all that late, but the winter days were short. If she'd been thinking, she would have flown in earlier so she could see the surrounding landscape. It was completely dark out and she couldn't see a thing except the lamps illuminating the highway.

As they sped along the interstate, Delaine felt a strange mix of apprehension and giddiness. She called out across the psychic bond she shared with her spirit guide and Sapa immediately came to the forefront of her mind. The black lioness was always in her head, able to communicate thoughts and feelings. When directly summoned, Delaine could actually see the image of the big cat behind her eyes and even call her onto this plane in a physical form. It was pretty neat to watch the expressions cross Sapa's face when she'd been summoned in the middle of pouncing on some imaginary prey. But tonight, the big cat felt Delaine's anxiety and sought to comfort her charge.

Do not be afraid. You will be happy here, and I will always be with you, Sapa said calmly.

'Of course,' Delaine pushed her thoughts to her lifelong companion. 'But this is the first time in years I've been off on my own with no children, no husband. I don't know where anything is, don't know anyone here except Pam. And what about this guy I'm supposed to get the goods on? What's his name? Baker?'

You will be successful, as you have always been.

Delaine basked in the warmth and acceptance Sapa sent along the bond. She drifted into a light doze and the lioness retreated to a small corner of her mind.

They were both snapped out of sleep by the sound of

Timmons' voice ringing through the limo's intercom.

Ah, we have arrived. Our new home is fit for the princess you are.

Delaine blushed. Sapa had such a way with words.

The limo pulled into a paved half circle driveway on a wide, quiet street. The outside lights were on and Delaine's mouth dropped open as she gazed at her new home through the window of the car. They'd arrived, all right. She'd lived in a nice house in Denver, but nothing like this. This was a large executive mini-mansion. Absolutely breathtaking, it was two stories of beautifully laid brick, with two sets of stairs that led up either side of a wide columned porch. The nearest house seemed half a block down the well-lit, tree-lined street.

'Wow, Sapa, this is amazing. I can't wait until morning to get a really good look.'

If you wish, I will lend you my sight so you can see the outside of the house now.

'Nah, that's okay. I can wait until morning. All I want right now is a bite to eat and a comfy bed.'

As you wish, Sapa purred on a yawn of her own.

Timmons maneuvered around a car in the driveway and pulled up in front of one of the sets of stairs that led up to the front door. Delaine inwardly sighed with relief. The car in the driveway was her black Jaguar, which appeared to have made the journey just fine.

They climbed the stairs together, Delaine helped Timmons put her bags in the foyer just inside the front door. She bid him goodnight and slipped a generous tip into his palm before she closed and locked the door behind him.

Her eyes roamed around the large marble foyer and admired the vaulted ceilings and hardwood moldings. Off the foyer the huge sunken living room, centered by a wide wood-burning fireplace, had her wowing. It was like someone had placed the living room in a beautifully matted picture frame, where the furniture, mantle and fireplace were the picture, and the steps down into the room were the frame, all the way around. And it was huge, perfect for the coming Christmas holidays. The kids would have a ball decorating the place.

Delaine kicked off her shoes and strolled from room to room. Her toes sank into the thick pile of the creamy winter white carpets in each room and allowed her body to appreciate the matching winter white leather furniture in the living room.

In addition, the first floor had a large stone floor gourmet kitchen, a beautiful dining room laid with lacquered wood floors and several more empty rooms. She'd turn one into her office and let the kids fight over the rest of them. At the top of the curved staircase was a landing that could be used as a loft or entertainment area. The rest of the upstairs was her bedroom with a large master bath from heaven.

She could live in the bathroom alone! The tub was the size of a small pool and sunken into the floor. A shower big enough for four people had a wall of creamy tile with two massaging showerheads and a rain-like waterfall showerhead between them. Two walls were made of glass brick with built-in bath benches. Done up in white glass and ceramic tile, miles of glass, gold and sparkling mirrors, it looked like something out of the ancient world.

Sapa purred at the opulence surrounding them and encouraged Delaine to relax and enjoy their new home. She unpacked her suitcases then made her way back downstairs to the fully stocked kitchen for a bite to eat. The fridge was full and the pantry was packed. It seemed her boss really had thought of everything. After a quick dinner she picked up the phone in the kitchen and dialed her girlfriend's number.

"Hey, Pam, it's me. The flight was fine and I got in about an hour ago."

"How about breakfast in the morning?" came the excited, familiar female voice on the other end of the line.

"Sure, but it'll have to be early. Tomorrow is my first day at the new job."

"You don't get any time to settle in first?"

"Nope, but it's not a problem because this sistah is hitting the sack within the next half-hour. I'm wiped out," Delaine said on a genuine yawn.

"Well, hurry up and get a pen so I can give you directions to my favorite breakfast spot."

Pen and notepad in hand, she leaned against the kitchen counter and said, "Go ahead, I'm ready."

That done, Delaine spent the evening exploring the rest of house. Later, she ventured outside to the back porch, leaned against the wood railing and looked up at the night sky to quiet her mind. Her head seemed to be everywhere at once, her thoughts bouncing from tremendous pride in her children who'd recently headed off to college, to missing the physical companionship of her idiot ex-husband. Then there was the sense of peace and fulfillment at knowing she could be alone and still be satisfied. After all, she had herself and her spirit guide Sapa. Moving to a new place and meeting new people was actually exciting, and this new assignment was the most important of her life. She had a dangerous target to take out and she couldn't wait to get started. The thrill of the hunt was an indescribable mix of eagerness and caution.

Despite her reeling emotions, she silently thanked the Great Spirit for so many blessings. Her lips tipped up into a grin. If Gary's trifling butt hadn't cut out on her and the kids, she probably wouldn't have accepted the opportunity to move to the East Coast for this assignment. Nor be in this fabulous house, nor reunited with her good friend Pam. She sighed. Well, thank God for small favors.

Delaine climbed into bed, checked her Taurus PT99 handgun, made sure there was a bullet in the chamber and tucked it under her pillow. She lay sprawled under the warm blankets and comforter then remembered the envelope she hadn't opened earlier. She bounded to the floor, headed for the gigantic walk-in closet and flipped on the light. She pulled her carry-on bag from one of the many cedar shelves and retrieved the envelope from the side pocket.

Back in bed, she ripped it open and dumped the contents into her lap. There was a picture inside of a handsome man with blond hair, emerald-green eyes and a too-perfect smile. So this was Brian Baker? This clean-cut, Opie-Taylor-looking man was her target?

Her spirit guide became restless. Delaine, so used to Sapa's presence, ignored the cat's agitation. She studied Baker's picture and began to plan a strategy to find out what he was up to. Where might he keep any evidence and what would she have to do to get it?

The longer she thought on the man, the more Sapa's agitation escalated until it flooded through the bond in torrents. Delaine finally gave up trying to strategize and quieted her mind. She meditated until she had the cat's full attention then summoned her directly.

'Come to me, Sapa,' Delaine whispered in her mind. The lioness stalked forward, her image visible to Delaine's eyes. Sharp incisors were bared and the fine hairs on her neck stood on end. Obviously something about Baker disturbed the big cat.

'What is it? What's wrong, Sapa?' Delaine asked, sending concern to her spirit guide.

The black lioness turned gleaming grey eyes on her and continued to brood but said nothing. Delaine nodded off with Sapa pacing back and forth in her head, a quiet, menacing growl resonating along the bond.

* * * * *

Baker walked into his office, closed the door firmly and turned the deadbolt. It was six-thirty in the morning and no one was around yet, but if nothing else, he was cautiously meticulous. He sat down, opened his briefcase and pulled out the file he'd been looking over during breakfast. He laid the manila folder on his desk, flipped it open and pulled out a picture of the new production process specialist being brought in.

Her name was Delaine Jeris, a technical expert newly assigned to his business unit to develop the new neuromuscular drug Zalactin. He would have to remember to reward the woman in Research & Development for getting him this information. Since the Jeris woman was coming on as a consultant and not an employee, neither Human Resources nor he had been involved. If not for his little bitch in R&D, who'd nicked the info from the dupe she was sleeping with in Purchasing, Baker would never have known someone outside of his "special circle of friends" was joining his team. Yes, he would have to thank...what was her name? Sarah Ann, yes that was it. He'd have to thank Sarah Ann for alerting him. A quick screw up against a wall should do it. He didn't have the time or patience for a slow one.

He picked up the picture in one hand and studied it closely. This Delaine was a fine-looking woman. Her résumé said she was an expert in systems, database and process analysis. Very impressive. Very beautiful.

A hand found its way down to his crotch and stroked his burgeoning erection through his trousers as he eyes moved over her photo. He noted the intelligence in her dark brown almond-shaped eyes and her flawless cinnamon skin. Imagining his fists knotting in the long natural curls of her hair, he leaned his head back in his chair, her photo in one hand, and unzipped his pants and freed his rock-hard cock.

Baker closed his brilliant green eyes, the image of Delaine Jeris etched firmly in his mind. He spilled his seed into one of the handkerchiefs he kept in a drawer for these occasions and wondered if the woman could be bought or, depending on who she worked for, sold.

* * * * *

Justin Cooley flipped the secure cell phone closed and grimaced at the new intel he'd just received. So a new investigator was stepping into his case, eh? It was a woman who was coming in as some kind of techno-geek. Her cover was to map out the production process and data sources for the new medicine that Brian Baker's team was developing. So was Baker her target? Justin had no idea. He also hadn't a clue who she was or what she looked like. But since he wasn't supposed to know anything about her at all, it was no surprise the information he'd been given was sketchy. His partner Derrick was trying to find out more. Justin would check in with him later.

Thankfully, the manufacturing and corporate facilities at Astin Pharmaceutical were huge. He blended in with everyone else, surveyed who came and went and who had access to what.

Keeping an eye out for this new agent should be easy enough. He was finally closing in on Baker. The last thing he needed was a newbie coming in and spoiling what had taken him months to set up.

CHAPTER TWO

Delaine circled the parking lot at the Arboretum Mall for the third time, relieved to finally luck out on a parking space close to the restaurant. She flew into the spot, jumped out of her sleek black Jag and hurried to the door. She was supposed to meet Pam more than ten minutes ago. Her fingers closed around the door handle when she was nearly tackled by a very excited female.

"I really missed you," Pam said with a toothy grin. She released Delaine and dragged her through the door to the table where their breakfast waited. "Hey, I ordered some of that frou-frou food I know you like, so eat up."

"Thanks, woman. Sorry I'm late," Delaine said, quirking a brow at her friend as packet after packet of sugar disappeared into Pam's coffee cup. Ick! She shuddered visibly then laughed when Pam stuck her tongue out at her. Delaine took a healthy bite of fruit, yogurt and granola Breakfast Banana Split. Her eyes rolled heavenward in appreciation then her nose wrinkled in distaste when Pam took a gulp of syrupy coffee.

"I'm so excited to see you, Delaine! Girl, I still can't believe you're here!" Pam exclaimed, squirming in her chair like a little kid with a new toy at Christmas.

"I know, I can't believe it either!" Delaine beamed, just as happy to see Pam. It had been eight years since the two women had left their homes in California. Delaine had moved to Denver, and Pam had been all over the place. She still couldn't believe they'd both ended up in North Carolina at the same time.

"So tell me again why you didn't like Houston?" Delaine asked around another bite of yogurt heaven. "You were there for, what, two years?"

"Too hot, too humid. Not enough gorgeous men," Pam jested as she leered over her shoulder at the butt of a nice-looking man being seated across from them. "I had a pretty good clientele, but it got old fast."

Delaine tilted her head in question and said, "But why Charlotte, of all places? It's just as hot and humid as Houston. Besides, last year you said you were going back home to Cali."

"I know, but I changed my mind. You know I've always wanted to live on the East Coast somewhere. I didn't want to live in New York. Too crowded, too expensive. But I didn't want to live in Florida either."

"Too many hurricanes," Delaine mumbled around the napkin she wiped her mouth with.

"You've got that right. So I settled for Charlotte. It's almost right in the middle of the Atlantic states. Close enough to New York to get in plenty of shopping and close enough to Florida to get plenty of sun. And, baby, the Miami strip is just waiting for me."

Delaine almost laughed at Pam's screwy logic, but for her friend, it made perfect sense. Pam moving to North Carolina because it sat between New York and Florida fit her personality perfectly. Sun, fun, shopping and hair were her life.

"You've been here six months. How long before you're off to somewhere else, girlfriend?"

"Well, I've always wanted to see the South of France. Hey," Pam exclaimed, changing the subject. The woman was like a gnat, flying from one subject to another and never in a straight line. "My salon is right on the other side of the mall. You only live about fifteen minutes from here. Why don't we meet here for breakfast again? Afterward, we can walk over to the shop and I'll do your hair, just like old times. And while I'm hooking you up, you can tell me what you're doing here without your husband."

Delaine grimaced. Other than her kids, she'd shared her situation with nobody but her boss Geri, and even that conversation hadn't been too deep. At the time, Delaine just couldn't handle getting into the morbid details. She hadn't wanted to think about how her husband had abandoned their family for the most unbelievably dumb reasons. He'd claimed she wasn't supportive around the house, but what wife would support a total nag? Especially when he'd nagged her and the kids around the clock. And god forbid there be a dish in the sink! Or a dryer sheet left on top of the clothes dryer. In all his selfish whining, he'd never thanked her for buying him whatever he wanted and standing by him in anything and everything he wanted to do. Not to mention the endless years of boring, uninspired sex. Funny, he was always the one with a headache. It was a wonder they'd ever had children.

She'd been too ashamed to talk about it before, but now she felt stronger. Maybe she should talk to Pam and release the disappointment and hurt once and for all. Besides, she'd known Pam since the Stone Age. If anyone could be trusted with her private business, it was the woman sitting on the other side of the table.

Delaine took a steadying breath and let the words tumble from her mouth.

"Gary and I are divorced, Pam. We've been separated for more than a year and the dissolution was final last week." She watched Pam closely, not realizing she held her breath until her chest started to ache. To Delaine's surprise, Pam looked relieved.

"Oh thank god! It's about damn time," Pam said,

sticking a finger up in the air while doing a seated version of the happy dance. "I never told you this in all the years we've been friends because I didn't want to speak against what made you happy, but I've never liked Gary. You gave and gave and gave to him, but he always made it seem like he was some kind of martyr for being married to you. It's about time you cut that loser off your apron strings."

"He left us, Pam," Delaine said, the heat in her voice directed at her no-good ex rather than Pam's revelation that she'd never liked him. When Pam's face fell, Delaine giggled at her friend's incredulous expression. She obviously hadn't been expecting to hear this. But Pam, being Pam, recovered from the shock quickly and was as pissed off as Delaine had ever seen her. But she didn't miss the hint of sadness in the woman's dark brown eyes.

"After all you've done for him, he left you? Left your children? I don't believe it! The bastard! That son of a …"

Delaine quietly cut her off mid-rave.

"Pam, it's fine. I've moved on. It's been tough being alone after so many years, but I'm fine. Really."

"I know exactly what you need. You need to get out and meet some new people."

Delaine immediately shook her head, adamantly mouthing the word no. Pam kept right on talking.

"Hey, I have an idea," Pam squealed, setting her cooling cup of coffee down once and for all to silently clap her hands. "There's a group called The Charlotte/Mecklenberg Professionals Group. It's where folks who are new to the area can meet other professional singles to hang out with."

"Look, I'm not interested in the meat market thing, okay?" Delaine said firmly, pointing a single finger at her friend.

"No, girl, it's not like that. It's a place for professionals, like yourself," Pam said, warming to the topic. "They do a lot of recreational stuff, you know, they network, go boating, dancing, take trips to the mountains and junk like that—not a teeny bopper, get-me-some-coochie type group."

The lioness had been content to doze in the back of Delaine's mind. Now, Delaine felt Sapa sit up on her haunches, fully alert, her ear pricked forward as she listened closely to what Pam was saying.

"Is it safe?" Delaine asked. The lioness and she both tilted their heads thoughtfully.

"Definitely. You won't find anybody like me in the whole place!"

Delaine's laughter drew the gaze of a few nosey folks seated at the table next to them. She pulled her outburst down to a chuckle and looked up at Pam through lowered lashes as she thought about her suggestion. So there was a place for professionals looking to meet up with others? Definitely not Pam's style. She'd be more comfortable at a titty bar. One-stop shopping, no intellect required. The woman had always been a free spirit, not afraid to tell a man she wanted a good lay and a good bye. Not like Delaine, who'd settled for less than mediocre sex for the entire length of her eighteen-year marriage. But now the divorce was final. Was there a reason she shouldn't get out and meet people, get on with her life?

"It's an exclusive, invitation-only group, Del. I'll try to get you into the social this Friday night. I put you down to get your hair done on Saturday so you can fill me in on how it went. Oh, and wear something nice. They're meeting at the Duke Mansion this time. Real swanky place."

When Pam pulled out the appointment book she never went anywhere without, flipped it open and penciled her name in, Delaine resigned herself to her fate with a sigh. She entered both her hair appointment and the social into her PDA and packed it back into her briefcase.

"If it's not your type of thing, how do you know so much about it?" Delaine asked, pulling a few dollars out of her wallet for the tip.

"A client of mine runs the outfit. She'll arrange VIP treatment, so no worries."

"All right then. I'll see you Saturday. And this social thing better be fun or I'm gonna talk about you bad when I walk into your shop." She smiled, kissed her friend on the cheek and rose from the table. "I'll see you later. Gotta go to work."

"Work? At seven a.m.?"

"I like to get a head start on things. Thanks for the breakfast, Ms. Pamela."

* * * * *

It had taken her most of the day, but she'd finally slipped away from the annoying Sarah Ann person from R&D. When Delaine arrived at work this morning, she'd been surprised to find the woman waiting for her, looking rather uncomfortable as she sat in a chair outside her office. The cute little dark-haired woman behaved as if her interest in Delaine was simple Southern hospitality for the new kid on the block. But Delaine was no idiot. The woman was shadowing her, but on whose orders? Perhaps her target, Baker, whom she'd met her first day on the job just yesterday.

She shuddered at the memory of meeting Brian Baker, a handsome Englishman with a chilling smile and the coldest green eyes she'd ever seen. The moment they met, Delaine heard the lioness growl deep in her throat. Sapa had kept it up the entire time Delaine was in his presence. And when they'd shook hands, the way he looked her over and held her hand much too long had totally creeped her out.

Delaine had always been a fair, "innocent until proven guilty" agent, no matter what. But something about this Baker character made her want him to be guilty of what he was suspected of.

She pressed her identification badge against the card reader and the doors to the elevator slid open. She pushed the button for the basement and scanned the hallways as they closed, thankful Sarah Ann hadn't popped out from around the corner. Removing a small silver tag from the hidden pocket on the inside of her waistband, she held it against the digital lock on the control panel. In seconds the little device deciphered the encryption and the elevator began to drop rapidly.

The labs were much deeper than she'd thought. When the elevator reached the floor indicated by the last button on the panel, it just kept going. There were no buttons on the panel for these floors and she had no idea how far down she'd traveled. She took a deep breath and steeled herself for whatever and whoever might be down in the subterranean labs. The doors slid open with a quiet hiss.

'Okay, Sapa, we're on high alert now,' Delaine thought.

I am one step ahead of you, Suta.

She poked her head out and looked around before stepping out. The doors swished silently closed. Delaine stood in the near darkness and allowed her eyes to adjust. She stood in what looked like a maintenance area. Little pathways led through and between what looked liked large water or sewage pipes.

Walking softly on the outside edges of her feet, her high-heeled boots made no sound. Halfway down the path she'd chosen, the lioness' ears pricked up. Someone was watching.

Shall I see who watches?

'No worries. As long as they stay hidden, we're all right,' Delaine replied. She kept walking, not wanting to alert whoever watched that she was aware of their presence. She flipped through a small stack of quality reports in her hands and busily reviewed them. She painted on an intent expression and confident body language that said something was important on the papers she rifled through. Anyone looking should believe she had every right to be down here. The lioness remained alert, but no one appeared.

The dimness of the little pathway gave way to a large

room lit by blue lamps mounted high on the walls. The room led to a series of tunnels that ran off in all directions. Which way should she go? If she picked the wrong tunnel, she could end up at a dead end, or worse, at the entrance to one of the labs where Baker was reported to spend most of his time. He wasn't supposed to be down here this early in the morning but she couldn't be sure.

'Come to me, Sapa. I need your guidance.' She silently called the great cat onto this plane, and the large body of the black mountain lion shimmered into existence.

Delaine would never get used to how big Sapa was. The top of her muscular back was higher than Delaine's waist when she reached out to ruffle the soft, wiry hair between the lioness' ears, glad no one else could hear or see the big cat, even in her physical form.

'Sapa, I don't know which way to go,' Delaine said softly into her mind. Immediately the hunter rose up, calm and sure of her power, ready to aid her charge.

Take what I offer, Sapa spoke along the bond.

The black cat lent Delaine her keen sense of sight, smell and hearing then shimmered away. The aura of the lioness prowled ahead and explored each passageway. Within moments, her thoughts flashed through the bond, telling Delaine which way was clear before fading away.

Delaine took off at a silent clip down the tunnel farthest to her right.

* * * * *

What the hell is she doing down here? Justin wondered as he watched Delaine make her way through the maze of pipes and pathways. She had to be lost. In fact, he couldn't think of a single female on the list of those allowed into The Vault. Hell, he wasn't even supposed to be down here. He had an hour, correction, forty-five minutes, to get back up to the locker room and slip the badge and encryption key back into the lab coat pocket of the scientist he'd nicked it from.

He remained in the shadows, hidden behind one of the

large steel and PVC units that delivered fresh air, electricity and water to these floors. Her height was average, but that's where average stopped. Her features were exquisite, her skin smooth and clear. Even in the dim lighting her dark brown eyes held a depth of intelligence and ruthlessness that caused his lips to draw down in a pensive frown. What caused a woman this fine to have a look like that in her eyes? Like she was after someone, and if the person was smart, they'd be running for the hills.

He let her pass by and then poked his head out from behind his hiding place to get a good look. He almost gave himself away.

Dayum! He exclaimed silently, his eyes glued to her firm, round butt. His mouth fell open as he watched her move into the room that led to the maze of tunnels. He could tell she was athletic by the nicely formed biceps and shoulders under the fine gauge of her coral pink short-sleeved top. The contrast of her tasteful sweater against her mocha skin made him think of chocolate-covered strawberries.

But fine or not, he'd better find out who she was and what she was doing in The Vault. Was she the investigator he was looking for?

The beauty disappeared down one of the tunnels off to the right that led to the quality lab for Baker's secret little projects. As soon as she rounded the corner and disappeared from sight, Justin popped open his secure cell phone and dialed.

"Derrick, it's me. We might have a little problem."

* * * * *

"Mr. Baker, I'm so sorry. I followed her to the ladies room on the fourth floor then I lost her. I tried to keep an eye on her, I swear I did."

Sarah Ann flinched when he pierced her with a malevolent glare. Such a wicked look shouldn't have been possible from such a handsome man. Blond hair, green eyes, perfect white teeth. And brilliant. She was surprised to realize she didn't even like him, and hated herself for needing him.

"You know, Sarah Ann," Baker said, rising and circling around his desk to stand directly in front of her chair, "you're assigned as the R&D specialist to my project. If you can't carry out simple tasks then perhaps I should have your boss assign you to someone else." He almost smiled when she blanched.

"I know I failed, Mr. Baker, but please… I-I'll do anything. Please, can I have some, Mr. Baker? Just a little?"

"What will you give me? I couldn't possibly let you have it for failure," Baker sighed nonchalantly, knowing exactly what he would get for his high-grade pharmaceutical candy.

He smirked when she dropped to her knees and tore frantically at the belt holding up his classic cut wool trousers. In seconds she had his limp cock in her hands and plunged her mouth down over him. He stroked her hair and said, "Perhaps just a little bit. Only good girls get a full dose."

Sarah Ann removed her mouth from his stiffening cock, her eyes wide with need.

"I can be a good girl, Mr. Baker. I swear I can!"

He thrust a hand roughly into her hair, tightened his fingers at her scalp and snatched her head backward, effectively quieting her too-loud pleas.

He snarled directly into her face, "Prove it."

She was off her knees in a flash. Baker looked down at her bobbing head and gasped as she stroked him expertly with lips and tongue. Her cheeks hollowed as she took him so far down her throat, he felt his engorged head bump against her tonsils. He kept hold of her hair, driving himself brutally into the back of her throat over and over, until his balls tightened and the tips of his toes start to tingle.

Just the sight of her swollen, wet lips wrapped around his shaft turned him on more than the tongue that stroked his length. Her mouth made him think of another pair of wet, glistening lips he'd much rather slide between. Suddenly he pulled away, ignoring the confusion in her wide eyes as she looked up at him.

Without bothering to tuck himself back into his pants, he strode across the room to a line of several dark pine file cabinets fitted into the wall of the elegantly appointed office. He reached into one of the drawers, opened a small safe hidden in the bottom and retrieved a small brown bottle. From it came half of a single tiny pink tablet,, the remainder, of which he put back into the bottle and secured in the safe. The little pink half-tablet teetered on the edge of his finger. Sarah Ann watched it hungrily as he approached.

"Remove your clothes," he commanded blandly, not really caring whether she obeyed or not.

Baker watched through hooded eyes as she stood and yanked off her sterile white lab coat and tossed it on the floor. His lips twitched up into a sardonic smile when the chit almost ripped her blouse and the buttons on her pants in her haste. She had a gorgeous body. A bit short for his tastes, but what she lacked in height was made up for with lush, full breasts, a tight hot cunt and a willingness to do any nasty, gutter trash sex act he wanted. And she was a good scientist. Expendable, but good.

When she was completely naked, he gave his next instruction.

"Sit on the desk and spread your legs."

He stood between her thighs and raised his hand. She automatically opened her mouth and lifted her tongue, sighing as the little piece of tablet was placed underneath. Baker took a step back, dug a small stopwatch and notepad out of his lab coat pocket and marked down the exact second the reaction began. He watched closely as her eyes glazed over slightly. Her breathing deepened, her small hands smoothed up and down her body, finally settling on her sensitive breasts. She squeezed them softly at first then brutally as she threw her head back on a ragged moan. Her fingers tweaked and twisted the hard, elongated nipples until they were swollen and red. She keened pitifully while her legs opened and closed as her clit swelled rapidly, painfully.

Thirty seconds this time. Baker was impressed with the progress he'd made in how quickly the drug began to work. He set the watch down on the dark wood top of his large desk and stepped closer to the writhing feast laid out before him. He was glad he'd had the foresight to cover the desktop with a thin sheet of plastic. It simply wouldn't do for Sarah Ann's juices to ruin the fine lacquered finish.

"Sink your fingers into that wet pussy and spread some of your cream over your ass."

Her limbs trembled uncontrollably as she obeyed, spreading her own dewy liquid over herself. Baker's eyebrow lifted at the unexpected turn of events—the trembling was new. Somehow, the effect of the drug had escalated. He'd have to look into that.

Sarah Ann shook, whimpered and undulated her hips, begging, ready and willing to have him any way he would take her.

"Please, Mr. Baker!"

"Are you sure you're ready?" he asked sarcastically, teasing the very tip of his throbbing cock up and down the length of her weeping slit. He didn't care whether she was ready or not. Neither did Sarah Ann. The drug saw to that.

"Yes, yes I'm ready. Now, please."

Her pussy leaked so much, her juices ran down around her ass to coat the tiny opening more. He raised her legs over his shoulders and pushed against the tight, slick hole, gasping when the head popped past her sphincter. She ground down hard and tried to impale herself on him, but he pulled back each time so just the tip remained inside. He held her firmly by her hips, dipped his head and sucked one of her breasts with hard, rough strokes of his tongue until he felt her pussy flutter through the thin barrier between him and her cunt. Just as he bit down on her nipple, he plunged and sunk deep.

She screamed. The pain tore into her, pushed away the haze of the drug for a moment as he ravaged her ass. A part of her brain was thankful he wasn't all that big, disgusted that she gave herself to such a devious man, let alone spy and risk her career for him. Another part of her, the part affected by the drug she craved, didn't care about the pain or the consequences. That part only wanted to be pounded by a hard cock until her eyebrows burned.

Baker continued to pump in and out while he observed the mental tug-of-war going on behind Sarah Ann's eyes. He was pleased when the drug won the argument. A blond brow shot up when Sarah Ann sank her own fingers into her pussy, stuffing her sex as he filled her ass. The extra stimulation of her fingers against his rod triggered his own release. His head fell back on a shallow gasp as he pumped into her once, twice more, and blasted his seed deep.

The drug was more potent than the last lab tests confirmed. The woman had come four times to his one and still begged for more. He pulled out of her with a plop, cleaned himself with a wet sanitary wipe from his desk drawer and tucked himself back into his pants. He tossed a bottle of sterilizing solution and a roll of paper towels onto the desk next to her naked thighs.

"Clean my desk, get dressed and get out," he called over his shoulder, stopping at the file cabinet again. A strong antibiotic was in order seeing he'd taken Sarah Ann's backside without a condom. He popped a dose of Zithromax penicillin, locked the cabinet and walked out. He didn't bother to lock the office door behind him.

Sarah Ann ignored the bottle of sterilizing solution and frantically pulled and rubbed her clit until she exploded against her fingers three more times. When her legs steadied enough to hold her weight, she slid off the desk and cleaned it and herself. Once dressed, she slipped out of his office and practically ran back to her cubicle in the

Research department.

The whole episode had taken less than fifteen minutes.

CHAPTER THREE

Pam had been right. The Duke Mansion was definitely high class. Delaine stoically oooh'd and aaah'd as she walked up the front stairs of the columned entrance and across the expansive patios. Once inside, she blended in with a few other ladies as she walked through the large French doors. She admired the historic paintings and tapestries on the walls until they reached the entrance of a soaring double foyer where a good-sized crowd merged into a growing line. Obviously this was the place to be on a Friday night.

A smartly dressed, balding gentleman walked down the long line and through the crowd, checking names against a list. Delaine was so far down the line, one more step and she'd be practically outside. She mentally kicked herself for not coming a few minutes earlier. When the man reached her, he checked her name twice before giving a tight-lipped smile.

"Pardon me, madam. You are not required to wait in line. If you would follow me please?" He extended his arm and personally escorted her forward to the great hall. Delaine made a mental note to thank Pam for hooking her up.

An attendant in jet-black livery retrieved her from the great hall and led her to an elegant dining room. He waited while she slipped her heavy wool cloak off her shoulders and handed it to the woman manning the coat check at the door. He then showed her to one of many small round tables, the perfect size for four people and a full-course meal. She ordered a glass of sparkling wine and discreetly surveyed the poised and professional men and women filling the room.

She wasn't sure why, but as her tablemates for the evening were seated, she grew nervous. It wasn't like she'd never found herself in a group of veritable strangers before. Her job required her to frequently acquaint herself with people she didn't know, get into their circle, obtain information they had no intention of giving her and get out. But this wasn't work. This was no mission. Work, Gary and her kids had been her life, and she hadn't been out to play as herself in a long time. Perhaps the fact that this particular soiree was for pleasure rather than work had her uncomfortable in her true skin. Or was something else rattling her cage?

'Sapa?'

I am here. Why are you concerned? There is no danger here.

'I don't know why I'm nervous. I feel like something is going to happen, or someone is watching.'

It is the latter.

And that's all Delaine could get out of the damned cat.

* * * * *

Justin looked up from the Earl Grey tea he was drinking and almost choked. The woman he'd seen down in The Vault a few days ago was being escorted to one of the dinner tables across the room. Her table filled up quickly with other women, but none as gorgeous as her. She seemed to hold herself apart, observing rather than participating while the others at her table introduced themselves, ordered their dinner and chatted. He was sure the guy and two ladies at his own table were mingling as well, but he tuned them out as soon as he'd laid eyes on the beauty across the room.

He set his cup down, leaned back in his chair and stared long and hard. Damn she was sexy. There was confidence in the set of her shoulders, just as he'd seen in the few seconds he'd watched her before she disappeared down the tunnel in The Vault.

Her little black dress, high-heeled pumps with matching leather handbag and upswept hair all oozed class and femininity, but her strong legs and toned arms screamed "fighter". Her natural curls were swept up into an elegant chignon, with wisps curling around her face and down her neck. Justin even liked the shade of lipstick she wore. It reminded him of ripe Bing cherries and complimented her dark skin.

Her mouth looked just perfect for kissing, and anything else his mind could conjure. He had no business even thinking about getting with her until he knew who or whose she was. And her appearance here tonight didn't change the fact he'd seen her walking around in a place she certainly shouldn't have had access to. She either worked with Baker or she was the agent he'd been keeping an eye out for. He couldn't compromise his mission sniffing after her. But damn, he couldn't help himself.

He picked up his cup and took a gulp. The beauty chose that moment to look away from her chattering tablemates and directly at him. He raised his cup in salute and grinned when both her brows shot up a good inch. He chuckled when she craned her neck to look behind her. When she turned back around she seemed genuinely surprised he still watched. He held her gaze until she lowered her eyes and looked away.

Justin reluctantly gave his attention to the waitress taking his order, or rather, trying to take his order. She cleared her throat for the third time and asked him again what he wished to eat. With emphasis on the word eat, the waitress' eyes slid boldly over his body, settling on the crotch of his pants. There was no doubt what the waitress offered off-menu. His tablemates' shocked expressions had him suppressing a grin. The girl's invitation was blatant, but Justin couldn't have cared less. His mind was full of the beautiful woman across the room who was now completely ignoring him.

He ordered a steak, rare, with a side of mashed potatoes and mustard greens, then tried to focus on the people at his table. He was supposed to be getting to know them, but his eyes kept straying to the tastefully dressed woman whose dimples appeared when she laughed. Who motioned with her hands when she talked. And eyes, so mysterious and exotic looking.

A chime sounded, marking the beginning of the social. Until dinner was served everyone was expected to stroll around the room and drop in on any table with an empty seat. The point was to make a new acquaintance, chat a bit then move on to the next table. The beauty never got up to mingle. She didn't have to. Justin clenched his jaw, surprised at the impatience he felt at not being able to speak to her. Every time he got ready to make his way over, any empty chair at her table was quickly filled with another man.

It was almost comical to watch them time their arrival with the departure of the man before. Justin watched the I-want-you musical chairs go on until the dinner bell chimed and everyone returned to their original tables to dine.

He watched her smile up at the waiter who brought her dinner, then attack her food like she was mad at it. She'd seemed to be enjoying herself, but now she looked stiff and annoyed. Her back was ramrod straight and brows drawn tightly together. Had one of the men who'd dropped in said something to make her feel uncomfortable? If he found out who'd done it, he'd give them a little wall-to-wall counseling for upsetting her.

Now he'd have to wait until dessert was served to go over and talk to her. That was fine. He'd already decided that before the night was over, he would know her name and anything else she chose to share.

* * * * *

"Here I am eating a delicious dinner in a swanky, first-class mingling establishment, and I'm sitting here talking to myself," Delaine grumbled under her breath, hacking her asparagus into itty bitty pieces with her steak knife.

But you are not speaking with yourself. You are speaking, or rather arguing, with me, Sapa whispered sarcastically into her head.

'I am NOT going over there to talk to that man!' Delaine growled back along their bond, stabbing her knife into a steak fillet so tender she could have cut it with a fork. The lioness was trying to get her to talk to the gorgeous redhead eyeballing her from across the room. But the cat was clearly crazy.

You know you want to meet him, Suta.

'Who the hell cares whether I want to or not? There's no way I'm making a fool of myself. I did that for eighteen years, and I am SO done,' Delaine fumed at her spirit guide.

Pride versus opportunity, Suta Winyan. Choose one. He's interested. And quite tasty looking.

'Puh-lease! A man as fine as that, interested in me? Riiiiiight.' It was times like this Delaine wished her spirit guide would go on vacation or something, but no such luck. The attractive man had caught the big cat's eye.

A possible mate, yes?

'NO!' Delaine wailed in her head.

More than confident at her job, Delaine just wasn't that bold when it came to trying to develop a love life. She'd been with the same man since her nineteenth birthday. At thirty-seven, she had no clue how to play dating games, and there was no way between here and hell she was putting herself out there with a total stranger. Besides, if the father of her children didn't want her, then who would?

You admit the puny Gary person you were married to was right? the lioness asked on a sly purr.

Delaine bit the inside of her cheek to keep her mouth from falling open. What an ah-ha moment. Sapa was right. What the hell was she thinking, allowing that bastard Gary to make her feel unworthy and unwanted? She'd been more than good enough for him. He was the first man she'd ever dated, ever made love to, and unfortunately, settled for. But she would never settle for a mealy-mouthed, untrustworthy, spineless, selfish asshole again.

Mr. Handsome-As-Sin with the piercing eyes didn't look like he fell into the mealy- mouthed category. He was stunning. He must be intelligent or he wouldn't be in this group. She would never know if he fit the rest of the bill if she didn't take a chance.

'Okay, Sapa, let's do this,' she said, and took a deep breath as Sapa appeared behind her eyes, ready to give any aid Delaine might need.

Delaine squared her shoulders and pushed to her feet. The butterflies in her stomach grew kite-sized wings the moment she locked eyes with him. He didn't look away. If anything, he stared harder. The man had no shame. The expression in his eyes was primal, like he had an unsatisfied craving for something. So that's what lust looks like? Her knees felt peculiarly weak, but she kept right on walking.

She told herself to relax, painting on a calm facade. He stood and waited for her as she made her way over to his table. Lord, he was so tall and powerfully built. Forcing her eyes not to widen like a startled owl's, she took in the length of his legs. He had to be at least six-foot-five to her five-foot-seven inches. His gray fine-gauged sweater accentuated the width of his shoulders. A pair of jet-black, tailored trousers showed off a trim waist, flat stomach and super long legs.

Sapa purred in her head as Delaine entertained thoughts of sliding her hands over the well-developed deltoids and thick biceps that bulged through the material of his sweater. His wavy, dark red hair was tastefully cut, with the sides and back cut shorter to fade into a neat line at the nape of his neck. His eyes were the most vivid, breathtaking blue. Like perfectly cut Caribbean Sea gemstones. Jeweled topaz blue. Damn, she'd always been a sucker for blue stones.

With a slight bow, he held out his elbow to her. As soon as her fingers touched his arm, she felt a peculiar zing dive-bomb straight between her legs. Woo, goodness! Delaine gasped silently. Her painted-on smile faltered a bit from the intensity of the unfamiliar sensation, and Sapa purred and panted as though she was in heat.

Delaine lowered her lashes, sent a mental "cut it out" to the big black cat and then looked up at the tall, ruggedly handsome man. Lord, he was fine. What had she been thinking, walking over here like this? Her stomach churned and her thighs burned. Oh please, please, please let her steak and veggies stay down. Water. Maybe a sip of water would unclog the lump in her throat. Then he smiled and Delaine felt her barely-in-place facade melt completely.

The two women sitting at his table glared daggers at her while the man glared daggers at the two women.

"Time to go," the attractive hunk said in a voice so smooth, it made her think of Luther Vandross on a rainy night, sprawled out on a plush fur rug in front of a fireplace. Delaine prayed harder for her veggies when his eyes twinkled mischievously. He winked, and steered her toward an empty table in a corner of the room.

He pulled out a chair and motioned her into it. "Good evening, gorgeous. I'm Justin." His chest tightened with what could only be described as pure male satisfaction when her dimpled cheeks turned a sweet shade of caramelized pink. "Glass of wine?"

He ordered a glass of rare white merlot for himself and nodded in appreciation of good taste as Delaine ordered a small glass of their best dessert wine...Sandeman's

Twenty-Year Tawny Port. When she also ordered an apple tart for them to share, he tilted his head to the side and embraced her with his eyes. Skip the apple tart— he looked like he'd rather just eat her.

"So, what brings such a beautiful woman here tonight?" Justin asked charmingly.

"I, well, um," she stammered, but caught herself quickly. She forced her breathing to slow so she could answer the damn question. Whew, he was just too good looking for words. And Sapa ran around in circles in her head like a fool. Looking down into her glass, she respectfully asked the great lioness to quiet down and lend her some of her quiet, royal strength. Sapa immediately quieted and sent a flood of calm confidence through their bond.

"I just moved here," Delaine finally answered as calmly as she was able. "A friend of mine suggested this group was a good way to meet other professionals. I'm a bit too old for the meat market, wham bam, dance club scene." Whoa! Had she actually said something so blunt to this man? Perhaps Sapa had given her too much gumption? Oh, he was definitely turned off now. Good. Better to get it over with so she could go home and throw up then kick herself in the butt for being such a babbling idiot.

Her annoyance with herself quickly became surprise and then utter amazement when he reached across the table and dipped his finger into the whipped cream of her apple tart.

"I like a bold woman." His grin could only be described as sensuously wicked. And way he locked eyes with her as he licked the frothy whip off his fingertip? Oh lord!

She watched his tongue swirl around the cream on the tip of his finger before his lips wrapped around it and sucked the rest of the whip away. Okay, the upset stomach was a thing of the past. Her heart beat so fast she figured she'd just pass out and wouldn't have to worry about throwing up after all.

"So what kind of work do you do?" he asked, still eating the whipped cream from his fingers. She kept telling herself to stop looking at that long index finger as it disappeared into his mouth but her eyes wouldn't listen.

Stop looking! You cannot have a decent conversation if you are drooling, Suta Winyan.

Delaine mentally nodded, thanking Sapa for intervening in her major duh moment, and took a fortifying gulp of rich, sweet port. The potent wine tingled as it slipped down her throat and calmed her churning tummy. Justin wiped his fingers on a linen napkin. Good, no tan lines on his ring finger. She looked up to his face and her gaze settled on his mouth. She'd never seen a white guy with lips like this except on television. This man had full, Steven Tyler lips. Firm, kissable lips. Oh lord, she had to get a hold of herself. Must be the wine. Sapa snapped her out of her examination of his mouth.

He asked what kind of work it is you do, remember? Of course, you cannot tell him.

'I know, Sapa. Geez, I'm not that far gone.' Delaine thought she heard a sarcastic snort resonate along the psychic bond as she answered the man's question. "I'm a technical consultant," she finally answered.

"Technical, as in…?" he queried.

"Technical, as in pharmaceutical and biotech manufacturing hierarchy development."

* * * * *

Justin lifted his eyebrows with a perfected dumb-as-a-rock, need-more-information-please look. He knew it had the intended affect when Delaine chuckled.

"I work for a company that specializes in providing analytical solutions to pharmaceutical and biotech manufacturers. We help them map out their production processes in a hierarchical manner. Then they can retrieve data from multiple databases for any part of their process. It enables them to do analysis just like that," she explained with a quiet snap of her fingers. "My job is to work with my customer's business community and scientific process engineers. I help them determine how they plan to use their data for analysis then we can build the graphical representation of the process, or hierarchy, appropriately. Make sense?"

Justin nodded. He knew exactly what she was talking about, but he kept his expression neutral. This woman was alluring, sexy as hell, and he was instantly attracted to her. But she'd just confirmed that she was definitely involved in what he was investigating at Astin Pharma. When he'd sighted her in The Vault, it hadn't been an interesting coincidence after all. Damn.

"So, Justin, what do you do?" Delaine asked. Mimicking his behavior, she dipped her own finger into the whipped cream on their dessert then licked it off with a mischievous grin.

Justin's eyes zeroed in on the pucker of her mouth as her dark cherry lips curled around her finger. He couldn't decide if he should choke on his wine or swallow his tongue. So he did both.

Out of her seat in a flash, Delaine circled around the table and starting thumping him right in the middle of his back. Damn, the woman has a strong hand, he thought, wondering if he would have bruises where she whacked him in her effort to clear his windpipe.

"Are you all right? Oh goodness, my first outing in this town and I've already half killed a man!" Delaine growled, and kept right on beating the hell out of him. Justin's hacking cough turned into a raspy chuckle. She'd sounded so sincere, he couldn't help laughing.

"I'm fine, Delaine, really," he wheezed around a final hack. He held up his hands to ward her off in hopes that she wouldn't pound him again. Well, the physique he'd glimpsed when he'd watched her disappear down the tunnel in The Vault obviously hadn't been a play of the dim lighting. He smiled big and shook his head in delight.

The woman was a treat. The smile vanished when, all on its own, his mind filled with thoughts of his tongue sliding along her smooth cocoa skin to discover what this rich treat tasted like. His cock filled right along with his mind. Hungrily he watched her pretty almond-shaped eyes turn all soft and feminine, then widen as he reached out and took one of her hands. He leaned forward and spoke quietly, his fingers a feather-light caress over the back of her hand.

"Thank you for saving my life, beautiful."

Delaine settled back into her chair, her face on fire with a fierce blush. She'd totally overreacted to his little bout of choking, but here he was thanking her. And looking at her like she was the most beautiful female on the planet. His gaze slammed into her and those damned butterflies stirred once more.

She could only nod. His expression was so lusty she couldn't look into his eyes another second. It did funny things to her belly, made her want to pull him across the table and jump his bones on top of the remainder of her apple tart.

"Delaine, I know a little jazz club not far from here. You game?" he asked, not bothering to hide the huskiness in his voice. He watched her body language closely and her eyes flashed such a wide range of emotions so quickly he couldn't catch them all. His eyes followed her tongue from one side of her inviting mouth to the other as she licked her lips nervously. For a moment, he thought she might turn him down. Relief stilled an uneasy flutter in his gut he hadn't noticed was there until she nodded and allowed him a glimpse of her dimples once more.

"Wait here, I'll be right back." He left the table, strode to the coat check. From a distance Justin could have sworn she was mumbling to herself, but as soon as she saw him approaching, she stilled. He slipped the heavy black cloak around her shoulders and put on his own coat before offering his arm to her again.

She looked up at him warily, her brows knit in a tight furrow of suspicion. He hadn't realized until this moment that he hadn't asked which coat was hers but had simply retrieved the one his investigator's mind logically picked out—an ankle-length black cloak with fox fur around the large hood that said "class" loud and clear. He knew exactly what she was thinking. Softly, he said, "Baby, I've watched you from the moment you walked in the door. You're the only woman here classy enough to wear something like this." He fingered the thick, soft material at the neck and secured the clasp, grazing her soft cheek with the backs of his fingers.

* * * * *

Arm in arm, they stepped out of the dining room and made their way out of the mansion. Claim tickets in hand, the valets were immediately off to retrieve their vehicles, leaving Delaine and Justin alone under the cloud-covered moonlight.

To Justin, the four seconds it had taken the attendants to turn their backs and move off into the night was four seconds too long. As soon as they were out of sight, he gently pulled Delaine to him, just close enough for the front of her cloak to whisper against the smooth leather of his jacket. He leaned forward, his voice a deliberate and seductive whisper.

"I've wanted to get you alone all evening," he breathed into the soft down of her hair.

Usually ready with a smart-assed reply, Delaine's throat closed up and every thought flew right out of her head. Her hands lifted to touch his shoulders all on their own while she fought with the rest of her body to keep from rubbing up against him. He moved closer, blatantly inhaling the scent of her skin as his lips gently explored the soft contours of her face. The kiss that wasn't quite a kiss had her practically melting. Damn, it was so erotic, she barely felt the chill in the air as her body warmed from her scalp down to her pinky toes. She wanted him. Badly.

Justin gently rubbed his nose against hers. His nostrils flared as he inhaled her natural scent. She smelled like allspice and ginger. Spicy, sweet. He liked it. He rubbed his lips against her cheek, brushed over her mouth and nibbled along her jawbone. She wore hardly any makeup, skin so baby smooth he could stand there and rub his cheek against hers until she tired of him doing so.

He worried her diamond stud with his teeth. After endless moments of bathing in the sensual fog that was Delaine, he managed to string together a few words against the tempting lobe of her dainty little ears. "May I kiss you?" he whispered against her skin.

Unable to gather enough air to speak, Delaine mouthed the word yes, almost desperate to feel his mouth moving against hers. Her head screamed, Hurry up and kiss me already! She couldn't tell if it was her, Sapa or the both of them. Strung so tight, her whole body hummed with the effort it took to stand there and look like a woman halfway in control of herself.

By the time he finally got around to it, she was ready to grab him by the collar, rise up on her tiptoes and lay one on him. She'd never had this kind of physical reaction to a man. Neither had Sapa, so beside herself, if she purred any louder in Delaine's mind, she was sure even Justin would be able to hear it. Oh lord, she almost hoped he would say something stupid to ruin the moment. Give her an excuse to shut down and bow out. All this stomach fluttering was just too much.

Justin played it out for as long as he could, but now he couldn't wait another second to claim her lips. He slanted his mouth tenderly over hers but couldn't hold it there. It just wasn't enough. Pulling her body flush against his, he deepened the kiss like they were in a private room with nowhere to go but to bed. When she began to move her mouth under his, his arms tightened around her until she was wrapped completely within the cocoon of his large body. He groaned brokenly when she eagerly opened for him, allowing him full access to her lovely mouth. He tasted, teased and then plunged deeply, entangling his tongue with hers. She was delicious, like apples and fine wine. Her ready response made his thighs flex and stomach clench wildly with need. She made him feel...untamed.

A quiet uh-hem caught his attention. The valets had arrived with their cars. Damn, already? Broke the kiss on a sigh but couldn't resist another taste or two. His mouth kicked up into a half grin when she smiled up at him, lips parted, and slightly dazed.

Justin stepped back, admired the sleek machine idling at the curb and caught Delaine's unabashedly smug expression. She drove a black on black Jaguar convertible. Exactly like his. Yep, the woman had class.

He pulled open her door and settled her behind the wheel. "Follow me, beauty," his sensual whisper a promise of things to come.

CHAPTER FOUR

Delaine followed Justin to a jazz club about a mile from the Duke Mansion. The four-minute drive gave her too much time to contemplate her ridiculous physical reaction to the man. What was it about him that made her want to jump him? How did a man she'd just met turn her on more with a look than her ex-husband ever had with his whole body? This just wasn't like her.

Thankful for the few minutes she'd had to get herself together, she managed a small smile when Justin appeared and opened her car door for her. He ushered her into the club with his hand at the small of her back. She couldn't help tensing at the intimate contact. His fingers burned through her coat, sending an uncontrollable tingle up her spine. Damned traitorous body.

The place was large and tastefully decorated with dark leathers and leopard print chairs. They sat in an intimate corner at a table just large enough for two. Mauve linen tablecloths, the subtle scent of fresh cut flowers and candles set the perfect atmosphere for lovers.

They listened to the band do covers of some of her favorite jazz songs. In the middle of a smooth Anita Baker set, the hackles on the back of Delaine's neck stood at attention. She felt the lioness rise to prowl back and forth for a moment before speaking calmly but firmly to her charge.

There is an enemy is in this place.

'Who is it?' Delaine queried along the link that secured their bond.

The one you hunt.

Baker was here? Of all places for the man to be on a Friday night, he had to be at the same club she was. Double damn.

Excuse yourself, Suta Winyan. Take us to the ladies room.

"You all right, Delaine? You look a little peaked," Justin asked, concern etched across his smooth brow. His fingers sought hers from across the table and stroked the back of her hand.

"Oh sure, I'm fine. Justin, would you please excuse me a moment? I need to run to the ladies room." Heat crept into her cheeks on a blush when he stood up with her and kissed the back of her hand. Such a gentleman, drop-dead gorgeous, tall, nicely built... Sapa prodded her out of her reverie and she hurried off with sure, solid steps.

Delaine stood in a typically long line for the bathroom. The lioness prowled restlessly until she could duck into the first available stall, lock it quickly and close her eyes. She blocked out the sounds of the club, pushed the saxophones and deep bass far away. The smooth, sultry voice of the lead singer floating through the speakers in the ceiling faded into the background.

Delaine summoned her companion with a thought. 'Please assist me, Sapa.' The lioness sprang forth and a vision began.

Through her spirit's eye, Delaine saw a short blonde woman sitting in her very own living room pleading for Delaine's help. Then the vision flashed to another woman sitting in a chair. Her hands were tied tight behind her back and a large canvas bag was over her head. This woman appeared to be in a large dark room that was completely empty. In the background, Baker's face drifted in and out, a maniacal gleam in his jewel-green eyes. Then the vision winked out and Sapa was back in Delaine's mind, growling low in her throat.

'Thank you for your foresight, Sapa, but what does it mean?'

It was not revealed to me, but you will know when the time comes. I will be with you, my Suta. Now go, enjoy the rest of your evening. The one you hunt departed while we waited in the long ladies room line.

The vision showed Baker was involved in something sinister, but she'd already known that. The identity of the women and their part in this play was a mystery. These women had to be important. Sapa only shared these kinds of visions if there was danger. At least one good thing had come out of her little trip to the restroom—Justin hadn't been in the vision.

* * * * *

Justin stood as he watched Delaine make her way back to their table. He held out her chair and was gifted with a brilliant smile. She seemed to have a bit more bounce in her step. That must have been one hell of a special trip to the ladies room, he thought.

"I ordered a drink for you. Hope you don't mind," he said, flashing a smile of his own.

"No worries. Thanks." But her expression was distant, far-off. He caught a glimpse of the wheels turning in her head and knew he'd given her too much time to think about something other than him. For some reason, jealousy rose up in his chest at whatever or whoever had her attention. Probably not good, but he wanted focused on him and him alone. He reached across the table, took her hand again and looked directly into her beautiful root beer colored, almond shaped eyes.

"I love the shape of your eyes, the way they tilt up at the sides. You look…exotic." She looked at him like she didn't believe him, but he was genuinely interested. "Let me guess. You're mixed with Indian, perhaps?"

"Actually, I am," she said, impressed he'd totally hit the mark. Most people thought she was part Asian or Mexican or something, then took one look at her long, kinky, curly hair and were completely confused. "I'm black and Native American. My family on my mother's side is Blackfeet and Lakota Sioux. And a little bit of Choctaw mixed in, though I'm not sure how since that tribe is so far south of the others."

"That's pretty cool. We have a little bit of Cheyenne in our family, but it's so far removed I couldn't begin to tell you anything about it. What about you?"

"Well, I have an older brother who actually speaks Lakota fluently. I only know a few words," she said, deciding how much to reveal about herself. Just because she felt she could trust him didn't change the fact that they'd just met. "My kids and I powwow every summer with our adopted family. In fact, my daughter and I are both pretty good fancy shawl dancers and my son is a serious grass dancer. Won first place last year at the Annual Golden Powwow."

"Golden?"

"Yeah," she said slowly, a bit of unintentional "duh" in her tone, "as in Golden, Colorado. It's a town. You know, where they make Coors beer." She laughed when he wrinkled up his nose and made a disgusted sound at the thought of actually drinking Coors beer. "So you're a beer snob? Say it ain't so!"

His hand flew to his heart in a dramatic gesture. "I'm afraid it's much worse than that, beauty. If it comes in a can that doesn't say Coke, it doesn't get anywhere near these lips."

His lopsided grin appeared, and the butterflies in her stomach came out to play again. The damned things should have been exhausted by now. Did butterflies take naps?

"So what does get near those lips?" she teased and

propped her elbow on the table. She rested her palm in her chin and regarded him boldly. Whoa! Since when did she know how to flirt? Goodness, how many times was she going to surprise herself tonight?

Perhaps this man brings it naturally out of you?

'Shhh, Sapa.' She'd never heard the big cat sound so saucy. 'You're going to make me laugh out loud, then he'll think I'm crazy,' she growled silently, trying to keep her expression steady.

"So you want to know what gets near these lips?" he asked, giving her own question back to her. "Only the best, I assure you."

Their drinks arrived and Delaine burst out laughing. The man had ordered Shirley Temple drinks for both of them, and hers had an extra cherry!

The best? Definitely!

* * * * *

Justin heard himself talk her into a slow dance. He took her in his arms and immediately regretted it. Barely managing to behave, his fingers itched to slip low on her back and tease the luscious curve at the top of her ass. Arms wrapped securely around her firm body, his nose buried itself in the top of her soft curly chignon, careful not to disturb the elegant style. Nudging her chin up with his nose, he urged her to lift her head so he could kiss her then kiss her some more. Mmm, she tasted and felt so good. And when she gave him delicious slow slips of her tongue and little nips of her teeth, he got so hard he could have played nine innings with his dick. Damn, if he didn't get her off the dance floor soon, he'd come in his pants.

To Delaine, Justin's kisses were like chocolate—rich and addictive. She couldn't hold back her soft moans as he nibbled and sucked on her tongue. He pressed closer and she gulped. Lord, the man was hard as a rock and huge against her stomach. Feeling his arousal did wicked things to her body. Good thing her wardrobe hadn't been delivered yet. That little inconvenience meant a pair of granny panties was getting soaked under her little black dress instead of her usual itty-bitty thong. All hail granny panties! A thong would have been drenched and completely good for nothing by now.

They returned to their table and talked, kissed and held hands until well past two in the morning. As he saw her to her car, Justin was genuinely pleased he'd shown her a good time. Unable to resist one more kiss, he leaned down far enough to take one more kiss as she sat behind the wheel. Delaine responded hungrily, as if she'd never see him again and had to get her fill of him right now. That lip lock singed the hair on his toes and left him clenching his teeth, fighting for control as he closed the door and stepped away from her car.

She pulled away from the curb and his smile faded. He started his Jag and flipped on the secure cell phone link hidden in the dash. A few seconds later the beep signaling the end of transmission sounded. The digital photo he'd quietly taken of Delaine was sent.

* * * * *

"Hey, Geri, it's Delaine. Sorry to call so late but it's the first chance I had today."

"No problem. What's going on?"

"So far so good at Astin. I met Brian Baker. A real sleaze," she grunted into the phone, fighting with her high heels, trying to toe them off as she sat down at her laptop. "You're a genius, by the way. My badge got me access to The Vault. How you managed to get the encryption key to work, I'll never know."

"That's why they pay me the big bucks," Geri chided. "That, and getting your butt out of there in one piece. Have you come up with any evidence yet on what Baker is doing?"

"Not quite, but I'm working on it. I've got a tail, Ger, and she's slowing me down. Can you check her out for me?"

"Sure, send me a digital."

Delaine pressed the send button on the encrypted e-mail program and said, "It's on the way to you now. Her name is Sarah Ann Crosby," she said on a wistful sigh.

"What was that?"

"What was what?"

"That dreamy sigh you just let slip is what," Geri said matter-of-factly.

Delaine should have known better. Geri Studebaker had been a top agent back in her day. She didn't run the most secretive law enforcement agency for nothing. The woman didn't miss anything and her deductive reasoning was second to none. Hell, she could probably figure out what Delaine's motive had been for things she'd done back in grade school.

"You're not going to believe this, but I met someone tonight. Ger, he's so fine, and smart."

"What's his name?"

"Justin."

"Justin what?"

"Oh my god, I have no idea," Delaine said in amazement. A name, a whole name, was usually the first thing she got out of a person when first meeting them. She had no idea of his profession either, having just asked about his career when she'd gotten the grand idea of teasing him with that stupid apple tart. The end result—Justin had almost choked to death and she'd pounded on his back like she was tenderizing a tough side of beef.

"Just be careful, Delaine."

"Will do, boss. Good night."

Delaine shut down her computer and then walked around the house, checking security. Once in bed, she tucked her gun under her pillow and summoned Sapa onto this plane.

'Come to me, Sapa.'

The black lioness shimmered into a relaxed heap on the floor next to Delaine's bed. She licked her paws and replied, *Yes, Suta?*

Delaine hadn't been this wound up in, well, never. She reached down and rubbed Sapa between her ears in a gesture that soothed both her and the great cat. "What do you really think of the man we met tonight?" Delaine asked anxiously.

He will make a worthy mate.

"I just met him, Sapa. How could you possibly know?" Delaine paused as an idea popped into her head. "And why didn't you tell me whether Gary was a worthy mate or not?" Delaine ground her back teeth, agitated at having asked the question before she'd really thought it out. She already knew the answer, and Sapa, if anything, was straightforward and a lover of I-told-you-so's.

If you recall, Suta, I expressed dislike for the Gary person several times before you married him. Yet, I am your guide, not your master. You will do as you will.

"Yeah, yeah, I remember," Delaine sighed. The fact that she'd never shared Sapa with Gary spoke volumes. "By the way, thanks for the heads-up in the ladies room. Who was the blonde woman in my house begging for help? I assume the woman tied to the chair was a different one. What did the vision mean? Who are those women?"

I was not told or shown. But do not worry. We are never given a glimpse of things to come in order to hurt us, always to aid us. Now sleep. We must rest for tomorrow.

"Tomorrow? Other than my hair appointment with Pam, there's nothing going on tomorrow."

But Sapa only purred, her long feline tongue lolling to the side as she began to disappear. Oh lord, the lioness was grinning.

"Sapa, you come back here!" Delaine called. "What happens tomorrow, you stubborn old thing you!"

Sapa sent serenity and reassurance along their bond as she shimmered away to her quiet place inside Delaine's mind.

Delaine was asleep in seconds, her dreams filled with a redheaded, six–and-a-half–foot, gorgeous hunk of a blue-eyed man.

CHAPTER FIVE

Who in the world could be calling her this early in the morning? Delaine grumbled, rolled over in her bed and snatched the phone off the hook. "Hello?"

"Hi, Mom!"

"Hey, babies! How are you?" she said happily, bolting straight up in the bed, now wide awake. "What are you two doing today?"

"We're working in La Boulainge for brunch," said Tanna, her oldest.

"Then we're going to play a round of golf. Finally!" Michael declared. He was Tanna's spitting image, born only a few minutes behind his sister. Both were enrolled in the Le Cordon Bleu culinary bachelor's degree program, and Delaine was infinitely proud of them. They'd taken the departure of their father with amazing grace and rallied around her like little soldiers during that rough time. They still had a relationship with their dad, though by his and his mistress-turned-new-wife's choosing, it was somewhat cool.

"We just called to check on you. How do you like Charlotte?" Tanna asked.

"It's nice. Lots to do, plenty to see. You'll love the

house. Most of my upcoming assignments are on the East Coast, so I'll be staying here for a while."

"Will our stuff get there in time for Christmas break?"

"Yep. And I can either set up your rooms before you get here, or wait until you arrive so you can pick which rooms you want."

"It doesn't matter to us. Can't wait to see you. The next two months are going to feel like forever, Mom," Michael's deep voice filled the line.

"I look forward to seeing you too, sweetie."

"We've gotta run," Tanna said, always the diligent one. Shooing her brother off the phone she said, "We'll call you next week, Mom."

Delaine felt a tug along the bond. "Oh, Sapa says hello to you both. She misses you as much as I do."

"Hi, Sapa!" they chimed in unison. "Love you, Mom! Bye."

"Love you too."

Even as tired as she was, she was so jazzed at hearing from her children she couldn't possibly go back to sleep now. With that, Delaine was out of bed and headed to the shower.

While she lathered up in the oversized stall, thoughts of her children filled her mind along with a nagging guilt she hadn't felt in a long time.

Tanna and Michael still had no idea she was a spy. Front companies like Aegis understood that agents, especially those with families, needed to maintain as normal a life as possible. Since she had kids, and used to have a husband, most of her traveling had been limited to short take-downs where they were pretty sure who was up to no good. All she had to do was go in, get the evidence and get out. It usually amounted to a few days here and there with the pretense that she was away training pharmaceutical manufacturers how to use her company's software or help them map their production processes. Perfect cover for her high-tech persona.

She used to question why she couldn't share her profession with her family. After all, she was providing a valuable service by taking scum off the streets by infiltrating their organizations and taking them down. But after so many years of firsthand experience with the kind of ruthlessness these criminals possessed, she was glad neither her ex-husband nor children knew what she did for a living. Ignorance was the best form of protection. And Aegis protected them well. After all, Delaine Jeris wasn't even her real name.

The steam felt good, but her conscience nagged. She'd just met a fabulous guy whom she wouldn't mind seeing again, but it had been forever since she'd had to do the "hide my identity" thing with a potential lover. She cringed at the memory of how she'd almost slipped and told him her real name last night. With Gary, she'd had years to adjust until keeping her job secret was second nature. But what face should she wear with this new Justin guy? And why did she wish she could wear none at all?

'Come to me, Sapa,' she whispered to her best friend and guide.

I am here, Suta, but I will not get into that water with you.

Delaine laughed at Sapa's dry humor. She'd learned as a little girl that the lioness despised playing in water. One summer while visiting her grandma on the reservation, her cousins tossed a non-swimming Delaine into the lake. Floundering to stay afloat, she'd screeched for Sapa to help her. Her cousins thought she'd suddenly perfected her dog-paddling technique. What they hadn't seen was Sapa's big black back holding her head above water, trying to get her to shore with all haste. Delaine's threats to tell her grandma sent her cousins fleeing, while a very angry Sapa wished she could sink her fangs into their backsides. Never mind the fact Delaine only had to put her feet down to touch bottom. Sapa had growled, hissed and, to Delaine's surprise, cursed a blue streak until her supernatural fur dried out.

Delaine pressed her lips together as the lioness' corporeal form stalked around the large bathroom. A giggle bubbled out of her throat just as Sapa chose a nice cool spot on the tile floor near the sunken bathtub, flopped down and regarded her charge. Delaine laughed outright at the sound of Sapa's droll voice.

It is a dreadful memory.

'I'm sorry, Sapa, but it's funny. Now. At the time I was terrified. But that's not why I called you to this plane.' With that, Delaine stuck her face under the shower of water and groaned. God that felt good. Too bad her mind couldn't enjoy it.

'Sapa, what's going on with me? I feel so...unsteady.'

There is nothing wrong with you, Suta. Your name, Suta Winyan, means Strong Woman. You are, and have always been, a strong woman. Even now when you feel unsure.

'But why do I feel this way? I've never had a problem doing my job before.'

Performing your duties is not the issue. Deceiving our mate is the issue.

'He is NOT our mate,' Delaine protested hotly, not sure why.

And you know this how?

Delaine scrunched up her face and regarded Sapa like the stubborn little girl she'd been when they'd met. She rolled her eyes instead. The great hunter lay on her side yawning, not paying the least bit of attention to Delaine's face. But then, she didn't need to.

'God, what is it about this guy? I don't even know him and I want to tell him everything. What makes me want to...hell, I don't know. I've never been affected by anyone like this. Not even my ex-husband, and I was married to him forever.'

Do you have to mention the puny Gary man? It makes my stomach upset and gives me the urge to eat grass.

"Sapa, you only eat grass when you feel sick or nauseous."

Precisely.

Delaine snorted at her spirit guide's matter-of-fact tone, then Sapa said something that rocked her back on her heels.

You do realize the puny Gary man hid more from you than you did from him, yes?

Delaine hopped out of the shower, sputtering like a drowned rat in a shower cap. Yeah, she'd known all right. She was, after all, an undercover agent. If there was anything she was good at, it was ferreting out the truth, even about her own husband. The cheating bastard.

'Enough said. Sometimes I wish I weren't the only one who could see and touch you. It would have been nice for a chunk of his ass to disappear and he'd have no idea what bit him.'

I would not have dared bite such a vile creature. Just the thought... Delaine's eyes went wide as the lioness actually shuddered and made a nasty gagging sound! *I must depart in search of some grass to eat. I am feeling somewhat unsettled.*

Delaine laughed as she grabbed her favorite aromatic oil and worked it into her damp skin. With genuine thanks, she responded, 'I'm fine now, Sapa. Thanks for keeping me company.'

Anytime, Suta, but do not fool yourself. Justin is for us. It is expected that you would want to keep no secrets from our mate.

"Uh, sure," she drawled, not giving in on the mate business. Not yet.

With that, her spirit guide faded into the back of her mind, leaving Delaine with more to think about than she'd had on her mind before summoning the big cat. Shower cap tossed aside, she strode to the closet to dress. The phone rang again and the tactical gear she'd selected from the sparsely occupied shelves landed on the closet floor. Thinking her kids must have forgotten something had her flying back into the bedroom. Her towel hit the floor as she dove across the bed for the phone like a third baseman for the Colorado Rockies.

"Tanna? What'd you forget, honey?" She tensed when a deep, sexy voice greeted her enthusiastic hello.

* * * * *

"Good morning, beautiful."

Justin? Oh my god. She wasn't ready to talk to him yet. What to do? What to do? Okay, now just calm down. The man wasn't standing here looking down at her completely naked butt, he was on the phone. But on the phone or not, her body responded to the smooth tone sliding over the phone line. Her breasts pressed into the soft jacquard comforter, which felt unusually abrasive against the sensitive tips. Delaine wondered if the small droplets of water on her back were starting to steam. She cleared her throat, bent her knees and allowed her feet to kick back and forth in the air.

"Well hello, handsome. How are you?"

"I'm great, but I'd be doing better if you were having breakfast with me."

"Breakfast? I…uh…" She had to what? Come on, girl, think of something!

"Have you eaten already? I know it's a bit late."

Whew! He'd just bailed her out. She guessed she should be thankful considering the state of her frozen brain. Wait, what did he mean by a bit late? Her first glance at the nightstand clock convinced her that the cheap plastic thing was lying. She couldn't wait until her things arrived from Denver so she could have a clock that was reliable. There was just no way she'd slept the morning away until eleven o'clock! Time to get moving if she was going to be on time for her appointment at Pam's. Damn, she hated rushing.

"I can't do breakfast today. I have a hair appointment in an hour, then I'm going to work."

"Where's your hair appointment?"

"Arboretum Mall. My friend Pam has a salon there."

"Well, why don't you meet me at Le Peep restaurant? It's at Arboretum, right?"

"Yes, but by the time I'm ready and get over there, we wouldn't have much time to eat."

"You're not just blowing me off, are you?" Justin asked directly but playfully.

"Oh please!" Delaine laughed. "I might have taken the time back when I was twenty, but now, handsome, I wouldn't bother to blow you off. I'd just tell you to go suck wind." Her tone was good-natured, but she wasn't kidding.

"I've never met a woman more subtle," he chided in return. "How 'bout a rain check?"

"You've got it. Next weekend?"

After two hours of sitting in Pam's beauty chair getting her hair done while spilling the details on the great time she'd had at Duke Mansion, Delaine finally made it to work.

She flashed her badge at the front door and stopped to speak amicably to the security guard before making her way to the elevators. From the numerous monitors on his desk the plant looked all but deserted, thank goodness. Nothing like surveillance on a Saturday afternoon. Humph, it reminded her of a bad song title. Surveillance was her favorite part of every assignment. So why didn't she feel exhilarated?

Because you would rather spend the afternoon with our mate.

'Hush, Sapa, nobody asked you. At least not this time,' Delaine whispered in her head, unable to keep the grin out of her voice. She received an answering chuckle. God, how weird people would think her if they knew she had a chuckling black mountain lion in her head. And the lioness seemed to understand her heart better than she understood herself. But there was no way between here and hell she'd admit it to the big, arrogant fur ball.

She put her game face on, stepped into the elevator and froze to the spot.

* * * * *

"Hello, Ms. Jeris."

Eewww! Baker's voice slid over her like oil. Black, thick, crude oil. The last person in the universe she wanted to see occupied her elevator. Sapa sprang to the forefront of her mind with a snarl, ready to lend her speed and strength should there be a need.

'It's all right, Sapa. I've got it under control. Go scout the building and see who's down in The Vault.' As soon as the thought was completed, Delaine felt the great hunter's presence dim in her mind as she took off to perform her task.

"Hello, Mr. Baker," Delaine said brightly behind a perfect smile. "How are you?"

"Fabulous, thank you. What floor are you going to?" His eyes practically glowed when his hand brushed against her as he reached for the control panel.

"Headed to my office. There are a couple of pieces of the process that are eluding me. I just can't seem to wrap my mind around them," she said in the most confused voice she could muster. "Thought I'd work on them while it's nice and quiet around here."

Both their offices were on the ninth floor, and that button was already lit. Damn it! The man's timing sucked. She'd been on her way to Research and Development one floor below. Since R&D took up the entire eighth floor and none of those people were in the building, technically she didn't have any business on that floor. She'd have to snoop later. And what the hell was he doing here on a Saturday afternoon anyway? From what she knew of him, probably the same thing she was.

The elevator doors slid closed and Delaine busied herself looking for something in her purse when the first image from Sapa flew into her head.

The Vault was empty, all of the tunnels that led to the labs were dark with the exception of two of the fifteen. Images streamed into her head of what looked like janitors or interns cleaning the floors and such. Excellent.

As Delaine continued to fumble in her purse, the cool

handle of the gun on the bottom of the large bag teased her fingers. When Baker's jade green eyes traveled from her face down to her breasts and then lingered, she wished she could just put a slug in him. God, the man made her skin crawl. Okay, she needed a distraction. She tried to engage in polite conversation, but it turned out to be a true test of her patience. He said very few words and kept his eyes plastered on her chest until he had the gall to let them stray to the vee at her crotch. Nasty bastard.

Almost to the haven of her office, he sprung a doozey on her. "Why don't you come to my office? Perhaps I can assist you with the piece of the process that's, ah, eluding you?" Oh joy, an offer she couldn't refuse.

They stopped at her office, grabbed her documents then headed down the hall to his. She'd been inside before but not while he was in it. This was the most help he'd been since the day she met him, and god knows she'd been more than content without his aid.

Okay, time to do the process analysis dazzle. Spitting out everything she knew about the manufacturing process for Zalactin, minus a couple of key parameters and components, she sat back and let him take the lead.

The bland expression on his face screamed bored, loud and clear, but his eyes flashed green fire. The man was either turned on or pissed off, she couldn't tell which.

He quickly filled in the missing pieces she'd deliberately left out and she gave him a big toothy smile as she packed up her stuff and left. Ducking into her office, Delaine wished it was farther from Baker's. The docs she and Baker worked on were deliberately spread out on her desk.

An hour later a quiet knock sounded on her open door.

"I'll be leaving now. Have a good evening, Ms. Jeris."

She looked up and found a too-good-looking Baker in her doorway. "Thanks, Mr. Baker, you too," her voice fading on a distracted murmur. Her head snapped up from the papers she pretended to be reading as she said, "Oh, and thank you for your help earlier. I think I've got it now." She motioned to the dataflow diagram on her whiteboard and flashed him a satisfied smile.

The second she heard the ding from the elevator she tucked her gun into the waistband of her pants, pulled her sweatshirt down over it and stuck her head out of her office door. The coast looked clear, but she backtracked past Baker's office just to make sure. She knocked on the door. No answer. The doorknob didn't budge. But she had the feeling someone was watching her.

'Sapa, is Baker in the building?'

He is gone, yet you are still not alone.

'What does that mean?' But Sapa didn't answer. Fine. She didn't have time for this. Striding toward the elevators, Delaine snapped open her secure cell and hit the send button.

"Okay, Geri, I'm getting ready to go down. The homing beacon is active. If you don't hear from me in two hours, send in the cavalry." She snapped the phone closed, flashed the encryption key against the elevator's control panel and braced herself for the plummet down to The Vault.

* * * * *

Justin watched Delaine disappear into Baker's office and felt his stomach knot up with disgust. Baker was the slime ball of the earth. So this is what she meant by "go to work" on Saturday, eh? A smile kicked up on the side of his mouth because it's exactly what he would have meant if he'd said it to her.

Even in her loose-fitting sweats, the woman was impressive. Nice wide hips, slender waist and an ass to die for. Damn, she looked as lovely as she had last night. Then she'd been all sultry and soft, a high-heeled goddess. Today, with her hair down in all those twists and curls he liked so much, sweats and sneakers, the woman was all business, ready to kick butt and take names. But still lovely.

Relief coursed through him when Delaine waltzed out

of Baker's office seeming none the worse for wear. Glad for the atrium in the middle of the building, he sat two floors up, able to reposition his scope to see into Delaine's open door. She appeared to be working. Her mouth was pulled down into a frown as she concentrated on something on her desk. She leaned back in her chair and stretched her arms over her head, arching her back on a yawn. Damn, that was sexy. He wondered what it would be like to be the one making her arch and stretch like that. His cock stirred and he cursed.

The scope now set on Baker's door, he watched the man lock his door, stop at Delaine's for a second and then head to the elevator.

Justin packed up and headed for the stairs. But not before taking one last look at Delaine in her office. If only he could go down and talk to her. But he knew he was the last person she would expect to see here. But he wanted so bad to see her. Was drawn to her until his throat clogged with the urge to run for the stairwell, down to the ninth floor and around the atrium to her office. Just to inhale her natural scent, touch her hair. And he couldn't do a damn thing about it.

For the first time in his life, Justin despised his job.

A quiet beep sounded on his earpiece. Baker was making a call. By the third ring, Justin pressed a series of numbers to kick off the tracer program Derrick had written to attach to Baker's cellular signature. Both of them would hear the call.

"Sarah Ann, this is Baker. I'm at the facility. I'm leaving now to make our appointment. Do you understand?"

"Y-Yes, sir."

The call was disconnected. Two more phone calls revealed Baker's plans for the next couple of days. And little did he know, Justin would be right there with him at each of his destinations. So much for spending time with Delaine this weekend. Strangely enough, knowing he'd see her when she came back to work made him look forward to Monday morning for the first time in his entire career.

Chapter Six

"Justin? What are you doing here?" Delaine's eyes went wide for a split second then her instinctive game face snapped into place. Thank goodness her body knew what to do because her brain had completely checked out.

"Hey, beautiful! It's nice to see you. What are you doing here?"

"I asked you first," she countered, unable to think of anything else to say.

"I'm a contractor for Quality Control. I'm usually up in the QC labs."

"Really? I don't recall you saying you worked here in our previous conversations." A grimace almost peeked through her painted-on smile when Sapa began to growl. And she was growling at Delaine, not Justin. The man had called her every day since they met and she'd purposely avoided the subject of work. The guilt was eating her alive.

"We didn't really talk much about work. You told me you were a production process something-or-other but I didn't know you worked in this facility. There are several pharma and biotech companies in South Charlotte these days. But you're a contractor, right? How long will you be here?"

Was that a flicker of guilt in his eye? Maybe it was her own conscience getting to her. Whatever it was disappeared so quickly all she had to go on was her own unease as Sapa's thoughts insinuated into her head.

You will tell him in time, Suta, but not today. Ask him to lunch. Before Delaine knew it, she was doing exactly what Sapa told her to. Now that was a first.

"Uh, how about lunch, Justin?" His smile lit up her world.

Very good, Suta. You have just made our mate very happy.

'Will you stop calling him that?' Delaine blushed in her head. Sapa just seemed so sure, but she just wasn't. It wasn't a feeling she was familiar with.

Ceasing to call him mate will not make him any less ours.

'Damn it, Sapa…' Justin's deep voice snapped her out of her private conversation.

"Listen, I just need to return these samples to the lab and I'll meet you…uh, where?" he asked.

"I'm parked in Lot J, Slot 2. Say, ten minutes?"

* * * * *

"Derrick, I'm in deep here. I just ran into Delaine Jeris in a secured elevator. I can almost guarantee she was on her way down to The Vault."

"How do you know?"

"Because that's where I was going, damn it. If she hadn't gotten on that elevator I'd be down there right now looking for evidence. And I have a feeling she's thinking the same thing."

"And how's that?"

Justin wanted to say "relieved" but held his tongue. The last place he wanted Delaine to be was down in those labs. The thought of her running into Baker down there made his gut clench so tight he had to fight to breathe. A subject change was in order.

"I've managed to keep out of Delaine's sight while managing to watch her all week."

"It's not your job to watch her. You're after Baker, not

a piece of Jeris' ass."

"Last I checked you were my partner, not my boss, Derrick!"

"Whoa, slow your roll, Justin," Derrick said firmly. Justin didn't miss the long drawn out sigh from his partner before he continued. "Look, Jus, I'm just concerned about you getting sidetracked. We've been boys for ten years and I'm just looking out for you, man."

Justin felt contrite for his outburst to his friend. Well, almost. Delaine was nobody's business, except his.

"I appreciate your concern, Derrick, but I'm all good. I can handle it. I know what my job is, but part of that job is to not get caught. If I rush this I could blow it. Listen, I think Delaine is being followed and I want you to check it out for me. I've seen a woman around Delaine, ducking in and out of Baker's offices…"

"So?"

"…and down in The Vault."

"Aw, hell."

"Yeah, my thoughts exactly. I've already sent you a digital of the woman. Check her out and get back to me."

Justin clicked the cell shut, dropped off the sample cart and headed out of the building to Lot J. He was amazed no one was on to him yet. If he was lucky, it would stay that way until he could get the goods on Baker and get himself and his woman out of here in one piece.

He shook his head and sighed. He already saw Delaine as his, and he couldn't tell her a damned thing about what he suspected was going on in this place.

* * * * *

"So where do you want to go?" Delaine asked as he slipped into the passenger side of her Jag. As soon as the door shut Sapa started dancing around her head as she did every time she heard this man's voice. It was damned disconcerting to have her spirit guide behave so giddily. Even when talking on the phone the lioness pranced, growled and rolled around like a loon. Amazing. Sapa's actions mirrored what she wished she could do. She looked toward him and his smile twisted her brain. Lord, could she even string two words together?

They pulled out of the parking lot and headed toward the highway. "It's cold as I-don't-know-what outside. Pam told me about this place on South Kings Street called Austin's. If you're up for some nice, hot Caribbean food we could go there," she suggested kindly. His startling blue eyes darkened to a sultry midnight hue, glittering as if she were the treat of a lifetime.

"Nice and hot?" his voice smooth as silk. "Yeah, I think I could go for some of that."

"Lord, you are such a flirt," she grinned back.

"Guilty, baby." His hand reached across and slid underneath her cloak to rest on her thigh. The skin tingled but she didn't flinch or pull away. His fingers felt like they belonged there, even when her breathing took off and her grin split her face in two. She knew she was blushing so hard, her scalp felt on fire, but she just couldn't help it. It might have been forty degrees outside, but underneath her coat was at least ninety-two!

'Sapa, send me some relaxation or something, quick! This man is sending my temp through the roof!'

"So how's your process hierarchy thing going at work?" he asked, his thumb tracing lazy little circles across her knee.

Her face fell, like she'd been doused with cold water. No need for Sapa to help her calm down after all. What could she say to him other than the typical oh-my-project-is-fine? She certainly couldn't say "oh, well my surveillance is going fine, I'm on to the bad guy and I've managed to elude the woman who's been following me."

"You all right, Del?"

A tremulous smile replaced her giddy one. All she could afford to spare him was a glance as she said, "Sure, Justin. Just great."

* * * * *

Justin could have kicked himself in the teeth. His question about her work had put her completely on edge. And that was the last place he wanted her. He knew what it was like to be asked that question. He hoped Delaine wouldn't go there and ask him—he didn't want to lie to her. But she was a smart woman and would probably pick up on his hedging sooner rather than later.

When they pulled into the parking lot at Austin's, before she could get out of the car, he turned in his seat, reached for her and practically hauled her into his lap. Justin poured everything into that kiss. Everything he couldn't say and everything he wasn't supposed to feel rippled through him as his lips unerringly found hers. He couldn't remember ever feeling so anxious.

Delaine pulled back with an alarmed expression on her face. Breathing ceased and he just knew he was busted. Why else would she be looking at him like that? Then the deep lines in her forehead softened. He leaned into her hands as the smooth leather of her gloves glided over one side of his face.

"Justin, honey, what's wrong? What is it?" He liked it when she called him honey.

"Nothing, beautiful. Just," he sighed, "a lot of things on my mind." That was putting it lightly. "One of which is when I'll have some time alone with you. Rain check, remember?"

Her smile twinkled up to her eyes and the iron grip around his lungs loosened. Maybe she hadn't figured him out after all. At least, not yet.

Inside the luncheon spot, she ordered for him and he enjoyed ox tails, jerk chicken, beans and rice and some kind of meat pie that was out of this world. And she'd been right. It was nice and warm, with the perfect amount of spicy heat. Just like her.

Back at Astin, he jumped out of the car, ran around to her side and opened the door for her. She gaped up at him, drew her brows down into a serious frown, then her expression brightened again. What the hell was going on with these cartwheeling emotions he'd felt rolling off her the whole time they'd been together today? They'd shared an easy conversation over lunch, along with soft touches of hands and sweet kisses. But when it was time to return to the office Delaine had been all over the map. One minute she was happy and smiling, the next she was wary and then sad. And seeing her in such a tangle of emotions just wasn't palatable. The need to protect her welled up in his chest. Even if it meant shielding her from her own feelings.

He stood in front of the car door, not letting her out.

"The weekend starts tonight and I'm still waiting on my answer." He was glad she didn't pretend not to know what he was talking about.

"Call me in the morning," her voice sultry and warm as she traced a finger over his bottom lip before snatching her hand back with a giggle when he tried to bite her.

Backing up a step, Justin watched her climb out of the car with fluid grace and walk toward the building. The wink she cast over her shoulder made his heart flip-flop in his chest. He tried not to watch her move away, but damned if he could help it. Even through her long wool cloak, her ass seemed to call to him on a cellular level, along with her smile, her charm, her strong but sweet personality. Damn, he could really love a woman like her.

CHAPTER SEVEN

Delaine groaned and rolled over on her back, shielding her eyes from the bright light seeping through the drawn curtains. Lately it seemed like she was always waking up to the ringing of her telephone. One eye cracked open to check the clock. Ten a.m. She swung her legs over the edge of the bed and sat up with a start. Crap! Here she was again with only an hour to make it to Pam's.

The ring of the phone was beginning to get on her nerves. Maybe she'd just hit the shower and let the answering machine get it. Thoughts of warm water sliding over bare skin caused Justin's face to pop into her mind. She wasn't going to call him, so she called out to her spirit guide instead.

'Come to me, Sapa.' Delaine wiggled her toes in the thick fur on Sapa's back when the lioness appeared underneath her feet, sprawled out on the carpet.

Wondering what our mate is doing?

"I am not," she denied weakly, knowing she'd never successfully lied to Sapa before. And she did wonder what he was doing. On the fourth ring she picked up the phone.

"Hello?"

"Time for that rain check, beautiful. Pick you up in half

an hour for breakfast?"

Justin! Damn, speak of the devil. Her stomach started doing the jelly-jiggle thing at the sound of his sexy voice. She thought about the way her name sounded on his lips and all the jiggle went bye-bye. After all, it wasn't her name. "Can't. I've got just enough time to shower, grab a bite then make my hair appointment."

"You spend a lot of time at your friend's beauty salon."

"So," she teased, ready with a retort of how all women needed to be pampered.

"I like it. Your hair makes me want to play in it."

Dayum! Not the answer she expected. And his voice was all smooth silk. Oooh, the quivering tummy was back with a vengeance. Sapa's corporeal form stalked back and forth across the room, her tail swishing in what Delaine called her 'happy ass'.

"Well, if we can't do breakfast would you allow a man to cook dinner for you?"

Her eyebrows shot straight up. "Say what?" Boy did that slip! There was no way she intended him to hear the shocked tone in her voice.

"Well, beauty, don't you think you deserve to have a man cook for you?"

"Is this a trick question?" she asked, smiling so hard she was sure all of her teeth were showing. Rolling over onto her back, her fingers trailed lazily over her bare breasts as she imagined his wicked grin and sumptuous kisses.

"Why don't you give me directions to your place? You can eat a little something while I drive over to pick you up. I'll take you to your appointment, go grocery shopping and pick you up when I'm done. I'll bring you back home, and we can have dinner. Sound good?"

Good? Hell, it sounded better than good. He'd thought of everything and Delaine couldn't find a single reason to object. And she certainly looked for one. Hard. Besides, no man was this damned perfect. Right?

Wrong.

'Hush, Sapa,' she thought, sending the ultra-weak reprimand along the bond, grinning too hard to put any weight behind it.

* * * * *

Justin hung up the phone in his living room, slipped his arms into the sleeves of his heavy leather bomber jacket and headed out. Once in the car he flipped open his secure cell, unlocked the keypad and hit the speed dial.

"Harris here."

"Derrick, it's me. What have we got?"

"You were right about the Sarah Ann woman. She's tailing Delaine, but we don't know why or on whose orders. We can assume Baker's behind it, but we have no idea how he would have obtained any information about who we think Delaine is. We think she's with Aegis, a front company for Interpol US operation. But she could be with any number of black ops orgs. Even ours."

"Uh-huh. Well, I'm on my way to pick her up now."

"Is that smart? I mean, she's being tailed."

"Delaine's got a tail, I don't. Besides, I've already made the plans." Hell, even if he was being followed, he'd still be tempted to show up at her house. He'd never admit it to anyone but Derrick in a million years, and only because they had ten years of trust between them. "This is hard for me to admit, Der, but I don't know whether I'm coming or going with this woman. There's just something about her. I mean, damn, the woman has everything a man could want. Smart, fit, beautiful. Hell, I even love her laugh."

"Her laugh? Are you on crack?"

"No, man, I'm serious. When she laughs, it reminds me of all the naughty things I did when I was a kid and nobody was looking. Deep, like she has some dark, sensuous secret."

"Well, it's probably a good thing you're hooked on her. You need a strong woman to keep your ass in line."

"Oh, and you should talk?" he laughed into the

mouthpiece. "So what's the plan?"

"Spencer wants you to concentrate on Baker. He doesn't have any problem with you getting with Jeris as long as you don't compromise your cover. Besides, getting with her may be the fastest way to wrap this thing up. Appears she's one step ahead of us, even though we've been working this case for months."

"How the hell is that possible?"

"Don't know. But there's also the possibility that somebody's outted her."

"I'll stick close to her. And as for hooking up with Delaine to use her to gather intel, you tell Spencer he can kiss my ass." With that, Justin clicked the phone shut and disconnected the call.

He'd been an undercover agent forever, and because of the hazard and secrecy of the job, he'd never enjoyed the companionship of a woman unless it pertained to a mission.

But Delaine was no mission. She was special. He didn't know how he knew, but he knew he was right about her. Right then, Justin made a decision that might cost him his career. It meant he would have to tell her exactly who he was and as soon as the time was right, he would. First he had to win her. Then he would keep her.

* * * * *

Delaine was ready when Justin rang her doorbell twenty minutes later. She opened the door and almost fainted dead away. Did men get better looking after a little bit of sleep? He smiled and pulled off his dark sunglasses before stepping over the threshold into the foyer. The only word she could think of to describe him was "yummy". He was dressed in a pair of worn jeans that fit his body perfectly—not too tight, not too loose. His leather jacket was unzipped and revealed a huge muscled chest wrapped in a black, tight-fitting Under Armour shirt, the kind the guys at the gym wore when they worked out.

She looked up at the ceiling and said a silent prayer.

Lord, please don't let this man take his jacket off. If I'm going to make it to my hair appointment, don't let me see his chest now, lord. She was so busy trying to keep it together, she didn't notice the sizzling looks Justin sent her way. After all, her dark blue Under Armour shirt looked painted on too.

"Did you forget something?" he asked.

"Huh?"

"You're looking up towards the stairs. Did you forget something?" He stepped close enough for her to get a whiff of his cologne. Oh, he smelled so good. She jerked back like he'd slapped her, ignoring the tilt of his head at her odd behavior.

"Uh, yeah, I just remembered that I forgot something," Delaine said lamely, knowing her words didn't make any sense but glad she'd left her purse on her bed. It gave her an excuse to flee the room. "Is it cold out?" she asked over her shoulder as she headed up the curved staircase.

Justin watched her glorious butt fill out her jogging pants and called out a chilly forty degrees as she hurried along. He bit his lip to keep from telling her how nice her ass was.

While she scuttled around upstairs, he took the opportunity to look around her house a bit, noting how meticulously clean it was. Sterile was a better word. No photos on the mantel. No pictures on the wall. He knew she'd just moved here and probably just hadn't had time to do any decorating. Or did she plan on leaving soon? The thought bothered him. Hell, he'd just decided to pursue her, no holds barred, and her leaving Charlotte anytime soon didn't jive with his goals.

He didn't know what drove him to win her. Frankly, he didn't give a damn. It never occurred to him she might have other plans. Besides, if she felt the same spark between them that he did, even the best-laid plans could be changed, namely hers.

He leaned against the mantel, his eyes glued on the

stairs as he waited for Delaine to descend. She made her way down, completely composed and distant. It was second nature for an agent to hide behind a mask of calm acceptance, and he understood that. Understood her life firsthand. Never having the luxury of getting close to anyone. Sometimes moving from place to place, either to chase down criminals or for your own safety. But the thought of her disappearing from his life after he'd just found her...Nope, not gonna happen.

A bomber jacket tucked under one arm, she stuffed her hands into a pair of navy leather gloves and headed directly to the door without even looking at him. An icy chill slipped up his spine followed by a tide of emotion that washed over him so completely, he felt like he was drowning in it. Such depth of feeling all because of this one woman? He could deal with that.

He marched across the room and swept her into his arms. His mouth crashed down over her, desperate to wreak havoc on her senses, needing her to want him the way he wanted her. By the time he let her up for air, one of her legs was wrapped around his calf as she moaned softly into his mouth. After another kiss, this one sweet and calming, he spoke softly from his heart.

"Delaine, I know we're just getting to know each other, but don't pull away from me. Don't shut me out."

She didn't answer, but the question in her eyes was clear.

"I saw it in your eyes when you came down the stairs," he said against her temple.

She met his gaze and looked deeply, trying to decipher the raw, open expression in his glittering eyes. Justin was the type of man to bare all, but he wanted her to see what he was feeling, to see what he wanted. As much as he liked her, he hoped she could give him what he asked for.

"Look, Justin," she said, trying to push away. He didn't let her. "It's been a long time since I've done the dating thing and I'm just a little unsure."

71

"I understand. Just give me a chance, baby, that's all I'm asking."

A double assault, she thought with a wry grin. Justin pressed her gently from the outside while Sapa pressed from the inside. Well, at least the lioness liked him. That alone almost made up for not knowing him. Delaine sighed, laid her head against his chest and snuggled into his arms for a warm hug. She could really get used to this. Damn. She would have to meet someone like him while she was on assignment.

* * * * *

"Girl, you are really feeling this man, aren't you?" Pam asked, her eyes wide as she questioned her friend.

"Yes, ma'am, I am definitely feeling him. Pam, he's smart, funny and not to mention gorgeous. And it's all your fault. If you hadn't talked me into going to that professional single mingle group thing, I don't think I ever would have met him."

"Hey, if you want to give me the kudos, I'll sure take 'em! So what's his name?"

"Justin."

"Justin what?"

"Pam, you're the second person to ask me that."

"Huh?"

"Never mind. He and I are having dinner tonight. At my place," Delaine waggled her eyebrows.

"Isn't that moving a bit fast, Del? I mean, what do you really know about this guy?" Pam asked, not really sure why.

"Concern about moving too fast? From you?"

"Look, I'm known for doing the dip-n-dash on a first date. But this is you, Delaine. You're the cautious one. The careful one…"

"The divorced-after-eighteen-years one," Delaine reminded her. "Hey, I've been careful all my life. What did it get me? And this conversation is getting old fast. One more guilt-inducing word and you won't get a tip, woman."

"Okay, okay," Pam conceded, raising her hands in friendly defeat. Besides, Delaine deserved some happiness after having her life shattered by that nincompoop Gary. Without faith, strength and money of her own, his abandonment would have been really hard on her and the kids. "I've gotta give you credit for bouncing back after that milksop you were married to, so I'll leave you alone about your new man. Hell, your ex is such an unappreciative pig, even I want to cut his heart out with a spoon," Pam said quietly, dropping the subject.

"You almost done? Justin will be here to pick me up any minute."

"Pick you up? What's wrong with your car?"

"Nothing. He gave me a ride then went shopping for dinner. He's cooking tonight."

A man cooking for Delaine? Wow! "He's cooking for you? Maybe I need to go to the professional single mingle thing," Pam said with raised eyebrows.

Just then, the chime on the door sounded and Pam looked up to see the most stunning, rippling muscled, well-built white boy she'd ever laid eyes on in her life. He had wavy red hair cut into a fade on the sides, a strong chin and piercing blue eyes. The man could have been the next James Bond. He held his leather jacket tossed over one shoulder, showing off solid biceps and wide shoulders. What was he doing in her shop? Whatever he wanted, she'd be glad to give it to him.

"Hey, Justin's here. I gotta run."

"Justin? Where?" Pam asked in a daze, staring at the gorgeous hunk walking toward her.

"The man you're drooling over, girlfriend. Snap out of it and take the rest of these twists out so I can go, will ya?"

"Girl, that's Justin? He's good looking and cooks too? Lord Jesus!"

He strode directly to her chair. Pam felt equal parts jealous and happy for her friend, even as she eyeballed the man shamelessly. He put his hands on the armrests and bent over to plant one directly on Delaine's lips. Pam finger combed the twists Delaine often wore loosely curled down her back, and still he kissed her. Nope, the man had no shame, not an ounce. He'd walked into a beauty shop full of sistahs and put one on the woman like they were alone in the dark. If her girlfriend had been chocolate, she would've melted into the chair.

Justin broke the kiss and stared at a dreamy-eyed Delaine. All his attention was focused on her as he spoke in hushed tones.

"Hey, baby."

"Hey, you," she said breathlessly, worrying one side of her bottom lip with her teeth.

"Almost ready?"

"Uh huh."

He grinned at her giddy, breathless expression and said, "I'm parked right out front, all right?"

"Sure."

He straightened and Delaine visibly shivered as his fingers traipsed over her bare forearm. Then she seemed to remember to be polite.

"Oh. Justin, this is my good girlfriend Pam. Pam, this is Justin," Delaine said, happy she had something to concentrate on, like forming words into coherent speech.

"Nice to meet you, Pam," Justin said with a friendly smile. Delaine noticed it wasn't one of the sizzling smiles he seemed to like laying on her.

Justin shook Pam's hand and left something in it.

"That's for her hair," he said, and turned and headed back toward the door.

Pam unfolded the paper in her hand—a crisp fifty-dollar bill.

"But it's only thirty-five for a wash and set," Pam called after him.

"Her hair is beautiful. Consider the rest a tip." He continued right out the door without breaking stride.

Pam and Delaine gaped after him, along with every other woman in the shop. Delaine snapped to her senses and hopped out of the chair.

"Girl, I've gotta go. Later, Ms. Pamela."

She snatched her coat off the rack and pulled it on as she made for the door in Justin's wake. She turned back to Pam to give her a hug and caught the strange shade of green in her friend's eyes. She quirked her head and stepped back, her hands on her friend's shoulders. "Girl, you all right?"

"Yeah, sure. Go enjoy your dinner. Put you down for an appointment in two weeks?"

"Yep. And I'll call you this week so we can get together for breakfast too," she said, kissing Pam on the cheek and flying out the door.

* * * * *

Delaine showed Justin to the kitchen and ran upstairs to change. She trotted back downstairs in a big tee shirt and pair of jean shorts to find him already busy cooking.

"What's that smell?" she asked, striding into the kitchen. He stuck a pot under her nose and she pulled her hair back and stuck her nose into the saucepan while he continued to stir. She sighed in appreciation, "Mmmm, now that smells really good."

"Homemade teriyaki sauce. I've got this covered, but do you mind helping me with the rest of this?"

"Sure. What do you want me to do?" she replied with a smile.

The twinkle in his eyes should have told her it was a setup. She gladly accepted the task to wash a head of lettuce and cut a few tomatoes for a salad. It took her forever to do those two simple things. And it was all his fault.

While Delaine washed the lettuce, Justin came up behind her to rinse green onions for the stir-fry. Then he needed to rinse the carrots and bell peppers, one at a time. Then he filled a pot with water and rinsed off the rice before setting it on the stove to steam. And each time he needed to use the sink, he came up behind her, pressed his chest against her back and reached underneath her arms to get to the spigot. The crook of his elbow teased the sides of her breasts as he moved whatever he was rinsing back and forth under the flow of water. Before he moved away to his side of the counter, he took a moment to breathe in the scent of her hair while pressing his stone-hard erection into the curve of her butt. Oh lord, she should have expired from his teasing at least twice over.

Her pulse pounded and a fine sheen of sweat broke out over her brow. Her fingers trembled and her hands were damp, and not from rinsing the stupid lettuce. By the time she was done with her small task, her breasts tingled unbearably, and she was uncomfortably wet between her legs. Here she was in an industrial-sized kitchen, with gourmet everything and more counter space than every display at Home Depot combined. But it was too small for just the two of them. She was so hot and bothered she could have skipped dinner and just had Justin for dessert.

Even with her arousal at a constant hum just beneath her skin, Delaine actually enjoyed their meal of chicken teriyaki stir-fry and fresh tossed salad with fresh balsamic vinegar dressing. Afterward, she led him into the living room where he left her sitting while he ran to the garage and hauled in a few logs for a fire. With a blaze in the hearth, they sat on the floor in front of the couch. Delaine paid no attention as one of her favorite classic action movies played on the flat screen plasma TV mounted over the mantle. She'd smiled when Justin pulled the DVD out earlier, but now she couldn't care less that James Bond was in the middle of laying some whoop-ass on a nasty bad guy.

Delaine sat sideways in Justin's lap, toes curled into the carpet as she snuggled into his big body. Her shoulder leaned lazily against his chest as he reclined against the couch. His masculine scent filled her lungs, enticing her to nuzzle into the crook of his neck while his fingers traced tiny circles up and down her arms.

Justin pressed light kisses on the top of her crown then dipped his head to plant light kisses over her forehead, her temples, her cheek. Her stomach flipped over when his soft lips traced the shell of her ear, blowing lightly. His fingers strayed to her shoulders and massaged the tense muscles there. Her breathing deepened at the insistence of his hard cock pushing up against her butt through his jeans.

His touch was tender and often, as if he savored caressing and arousing her. She took delight in the affection he lavished on her, even as her body heated and her blood simmered. His touch was magic. A deep, needy groan traveled up her throat when one of his large, strong hands traced the line of her neck, teasing each individual vertebrate as he worked his way down. His free hand slid across the quivering planes of her stomach and around to her waist to hold her tightly to him.

His growing erection told her how much he enjoyed touching her. It royally turned her on to feel him harden and stretch underneath her. Slowly, so slowly, her hips began to writhe, seeking more of the hardness pressing against her. Her eyelids drooped closed as body and mind accepted his sweet attention on a sigh.

Her breasts swelled and ached, the tips so tender she gasped with an erotic shiver when Justin's forearm accidentally scraped against them on the way to wrap around her body.

Oh please, please touch my breasts, she willed him silently with each tormented breath pulled from her chest. As her body reached out for him, Delaine felt Sapa slip completely away from her. On the verge of panic at the sudden emptiness in her mind, the bond vibrated softly. Sapa was giving her privacy. Privacy to mate.

Delaine lifted her head from beneath his chin. Her tongue flicked out and tasted the sweet muskiness of his skin, salty from the sweat she hadn't realized was there. His skin felt hot against her lips. She opened her mouth against his throat and allowed her tongue free reign. Licked and tasted with wild, carnal slides of her tongue along the column of his throat, smiling against the taut muscles of his neck when he leaned his head back with a moan and ground his hips up against her ass.

Justin leaned forward and whispered in her ear. "You feel so good in my arms, Delaine. You're driving me crazy, baby. I can smell your heat and I'm trying really hard to keep my hands to myself." His breathing deepened with each word.

She stretched sensuously against him and said, "I don't want you to keep them to yourself." Delaine reached for his hand splayed across her hip and placed it boldly on her breasts. She closed her eyes on a swift intake of breath as Justin proved he could more than take it from there.

CHAPTER EIGHT

Delaine was a starving woman, arching wildly into Justin's hands as they closed firmly around her aching, tender breasts. She wanted him to wrap his fingers around them and knead them like fresh bread dough. She couldn't hold back a long, needy moan as he found her nipples through her bra. He tweaked them, then smoothed insistent fingers over the stiff peaks. It didn't take long before she needed more.

Her back against his chest, she wiggled down between his legs until she was on the floor between his thighs. Delaine reached back and slipped her arms around his neck, stretching into him like the sleek cat who shared her conscience. Her oversized tee shirt rode up to expose the smooth milk chocolate skin of her belly and she quivered as Justin slipped his hands underneath the fabric, his rough hands seeking, moving up her body to explore the ridges of her washboard stomach. Long, warm fingers skimmed over the goose bumps around her waist and teased the top of her pants. Her hips swiveled all on their own, seeking the thick ridge of his cock through his jeans. He nibbled and kissed his way around the back of her neck, making her hungrier. She felt the clasp on the front of her bra snap loose. The second her breasts spilled free, he lavished them with attention.

"Mmmm, your hands feel so good. Oh yes, touch me, Justin," Delaine moaned.

Justin grabbed her underneath her arms and picked her up as if she weighed nothing, turning her around to face him. Settled her on her knees, her thighs straddled his and her hot channel came down directly on top of his straining erection. He took her mouth almost brutally, tasting her, pulling her into himself. He lifted her up again and his head disappeared under her tee shirt. The way she cried out when he took a delicious, dark nipple into his mouth made him want to wring that sound from her over and over again. Made him want to suck, feast and ravage her flesh until she trembled uncontrollably.

Every desperate sound she made evoked powerful feelings of possessiveness in him. When her cries became desperate, the need to be inside her right then and there raged through his blood without restraint. He released her breasts and wrapped his arms around her in a sensuous cocoon. He kissed her neck and along her jaw, grinding the steel bulge in his pants hard against her clit. Delaine held onto his neck as if she was drowning and he understood exactly how she felt. Leaning her back a bit, he buried his face between her breasts long enough to get his breath.

"Justin." It was a whisper so heavy with passion, it made him feel so untamed he wanted to rip off all her clothes and take her right there on the carpet.

"I have to make love to you, baby," he rasped through gritted teeth. "Tell me you want me."

"Justin, please." Delaine ground her hips against his hardness, needing to satisfy the throbbing between her legs. Oh, she wanted him, all right.

"Then tell me," he hissed, sliding his large hands over her ass, fingers pressing up against her weeping slit from behind. She almost came on the spot.

"Oooh, Justin," she wailed, "yes! I want you!"

"Stand up for me, baby."

She rose on wobbly legs and reached for the waistband of her pants. She jumped when, quick as lightning, Justin's hand shot out and pushed hers away.

"Don't...move."

His voice was hard, desperate. Delaine dropped her hands to her sides. He began to undress her. It was torture. Sheer, unadulterated, bliss-filled torture. His lips traveled over every inch of skin as he exposed it. Inching her shirt up, his mouth kissed its way up her stomach, gobbled up a breast on the way, then nibbled and licked a path up her neck, around her nape and down the other side. He found a sensitive spot where her neck met her shoulder muscles. He bit down gently and made her squirm and gasp as the knee-buckling sensations shimmied down her spine. Her shirt and bra hit the floor and he moved on to her pants.

Justin slowly moved the waistband of her shorts down a bit and kissed his way around her waist. Her stomach rippled when he licked her navel, so he did it again and again, worshipping her body.

He moved around behind her, nipped and licked the cheeks of her ass as he lowered her bottoms. Delaine shuddered when he gently raked his short nails over the sensitive globes. His teeth lightly grazed her flesh. Mmm, he's a biter. Oh lord, that feels so good. The grazing of his teeth was replaced by the sweet suction of his full lips as his mouth settled on her left ass cheek. Next came hard, intense sucking. Her pussy clenched violently. Justin caught her when her knees buckled. He kicked her shorts out of the way, swept her up in his arms and headed for the stairs.

* * * * *

He set Delaine's feet on the floor long enough to push the covers back. He picked her up again, laid her on the edge of her bed and leaned over her to tease and torment her with his lips and tongue. Nudging her thighs apart, he slid his fingers between her legs. He gave her a lopsided grin when he withdrew his hand and licked off the evidence of her arousal while gently easing the fingers of his other hand inside her slick flesh. She was a quivering mass of muscle and bone, but he was nowhere close to finished with her. He wanted to hear her scream. See her scratch the sheets off the bed. He wanted her so far gone, she would give him anything and everything he wanted.

He stood up to remove his clothes and Delaine bolted up in the bed.

"Don't leave me!" she cried, her eyes full of longing while her body trembled uncontrollably.

For a second he wondered at the panic in her voice and was even more determined she would never have to worry or wonder about his need for her. Before the night was over she would feel beyond cherished. Then again, maybe he'd tell her that he needed her so badly he wanted to lay a hurtin' on her pussy that would have her begging him to leave her alone. Instead he simply said, "I won't leave you, baby, but I can't wait another minute to feel my skin sliding against yours."

Justin's gaze never left hers as he peeled his shirt off over his head, exposing the wide planes of his body to Delaine's hungry gaze. With each movement, her eyes followed the ripple of taut muscle. He'd never been stuck on his physique before, but now he felt a strong sense of pride and prowess as he watched Delaine admire the power of his honed body. She sat on the edge of the bed and ran her palms over his large biceps, then across broad sculpted pecs, savoring the feel of the downy soft, reddish-blond hair sprinkled there. Her eyes traveled down his chest to a chiseled, ripped stomach.

He stepped back, made short work of his pants then stood and let Delaine look her fill. He watched her tongue travel across her lush, full lips as she took him in. Her eyes traveled down past his hips and grew wide as she stared at his cock in wonder. It jutted out from his body, huge, jerking with a life of its own. He wasn't sure he'd ever been this hard. The thick mushroom head was moist and weeping. If he wasn't beyond ready, his cock certainly was.

"Oh lord," she gasped, breaking out of the sexual stupor she'd been floating in. "You're going to kill me with that thing!" Survival instinct kicked in, propelling her body backward so she could scoot away across the bed. Her lust evaporated into uncertainty and more than a bit of fear.

Justin chuckled, but his need didn't diminish one whit. He grasped his wide base and stroked his length as he stalked toward the bed.

"Don't worry, beauty. I know what to do with it." But first he had to get her mind off the size of his cock. He reached out, grabbed her by an ankle and pulled her forward until she sat with her legs spread on the edge of the bed. Leaning down, he licked her across the mouth and silently smiled to himself when her eyes fluttered closed and some of the tension leached from her body. His teeth captured her bottom lip and worried it a little before pulling it into his mouth like a ripe piece of juicy fruit. Her arms wrapped around him, breasts writhing flush against his chest.

"Just lie still for me, baby. Close your eyes and let me taste you," he whispered against her lush mouth.

Delaine looked like she wasn't sure of what he was talking about, but she let him rearrange her on the bed. Her lashes fluttered closed as he stroked her thighs, encouraging her to ease back on the bed to give him room to kneel on the edge. Pushing her thighs farther apart, he lifted her legs over his shoulders. Then came the hot swipe of his tongue up her swollen cunt.

"Oh lord!" she cried and almost shot straight up off the bed, more than a little self-conscious and obviously glad she'd shaved down there this morning.

He lifted his head long enough to ask, "Hasn't anyone ever loved you like this, beauty?"

She shook her head dumbly, her breathing sharp as his

fingers played with the smooth skin just above her clit. His thumb dipped down and pressed up against the swollen bundle of nerves and her hips jerked forward, eyes closed on a strangled cry.

"Lie back. Relax," he ordered gently and then dipped his nose into her sex and inhaled. The delicious scent of her tender folds called to his blood until the need to please her as no one else ever had overrode all other desire.

"God, Delaine, you smell so good. Like cinnamon and spice. I need to taste your sweet, pretty pussy."

He then licked her from the top of her slit to the bottom, smoothing his hands up and down her quivering thighs as he dove headlong. Whipped his tongue across, up, down and inside her until she writhed and cried out in a frenzy of need. He moaned against her and deliberately sent a titillating humming against her clit. But when he sucked the sensitive knot roughly, as deep as he could get it into his mouth, she yelled to the rafters. Delaine grabbed his head between her thighs and bucked wildly, coming long and hard. But Justin didn't stop lashing her with his tongue, just kept at her until she exploded again.

"See how good you taste, baby," he whispered, sliding up her body to cover her mouth with his. The taste of herself on his tongue was such a turn-on, she latched onto the talented pink organ, sank her fingers into his hair and sucked his tongue like a piece of candy.

Justin broke the kiss, sat back on his knees and pulled her hips up his thighs to position himself at her entrance. He needed to feel her wrapped around his cock, needed to feel the slick walls of her pussy holding him tight. But first, he needed to hear the words.

"I need to be inside you right now," he ground out, teasing the head of his throbbing dick against her swollen, slick flesh. "I want to fuck you, Delaine. Now, tell me what you want."

Instead, she tried to shimmy herself up his legs and impale herself on his hard length.

"Tell me what you want, baby," his request was a tight-lipped command, barely in check.

"I-I want you."

"You want me to what?" Her eyes were wide with need, but Justin could see her starting to think. But he didn't want her to think, he wanted her to feel. Still rubbing himself against her slick heat, he made it very plain what he was after.

"Listen to me, baby. I'm nasty as hell. A total freak. I want to lick, suck and fuck you all night, but I want you right there with me. Hot, creaming and screaming for me. So tell me what you want. I won't take you until you do."

Delaine wasn't sure she liked this kind of control. But maybe it was because her ex had never exerted it? With Justin, it felt right. It blew her mind that she actually wanted to be dominated in the bedroom. She wanted to be ridden hard, taken. By him. But she had to be woman enough, bold enough, to tell him what she wanted.

"I want you to fuck me, Justin. Please, honey," she whispered. A little unsure but determined, her palm reached out and stroked what she wanted. Her fingers wrapped around his dripping, hard cock. When he moaned and bucked against her hand, she grew a bit more bold. "I want you hard and deep. Fuck me until I'm so hot, my hair is on fire."

"Guide me in." Eyes closed, he let her guide him into her hot, soaking wet channel. When the thick, almost purple head of his cock was positioned at her entrance, he flexed his hips and slowly inched his way in. He knew he was big and tried to take his time so he wouldn't hurt her. His eyes flew open when Delaine raised up on her elbows, put one foot on his chest, the other flat on the bed and pushed forward with all her strength. He slammed home and bumped against the entrance to her womb. They threw their heads back on a unified yell. At this rate, they'd both be hoarse by morning.

He leaned forward until he lay on top of her and then

gathered her into his arms. Skin to skin, breast to breast, he slowly stroked into her as he whispered how beautifully sexy she was. How much he loved being inside her warmth. She moaned non-stop, but he wanted more. He wanted to mark her, brand her as his. He'd never felt this primal with a woman. Tried to rein it in, but after a few moments of gritting his teeth against the urges, he gave up the fight.

On his knees again, he took her with him until only the top of her shoulders were left on the bed. Stomach muscles tightened as he clenched his teeth and withdrew his length until only the head of his cock was in her creamy, moist heat. He pistoned into her but gave her only that little bit. Her hips rose to meet him stroke for stroke, but he wouldn't give her any more than that.

She'd been so unbelievably full of him, reveled in the deep plunging he'd been giving her. Now he teased her with quick shallow strokes and Delaine was on fire, desperate to have all of him inside her again. She had no shame as she grabbed the sheets and ripped at them with her nails. She yanked and pulled at his body, trying to get more of him. Her head thrashed back and forth and her hair became a wild silky tangle. Every other word from her lips was his name.

Then she begged, and he completely lost it.

"Justin, stop teasing me! Oh, god! Please... please! Give it to me!"

It was over for him. He didn't need any more encouragement to sink back into her depths. In fact, he couldn't wait another second. He leaned forward, supported his weight with one arm and held Delaine by the hip with the other until she was tight against his body.

He plowed deeply until he thought he'd see his cock behind her eyes. Damn she was tight, and felt so good, so right as he rode her hard. Sweat poured off him and mingled with hers until he was wet to the scalp with it. He growled, swore, moaned and pumped until his name was one long word out of her mouth.

"JustinJustinJustinJustinJustin!"

He ground down and felt Delaine's wet heat flutter and tighten around him, milking him as he panted wicked words in her ear.

"Ah, baby, you feel so good. Come for me. Milk my cock and give me that cream." And she did, tightening almost painfully around him, squeezing then scalding him with her flowing juices. He came with a shout right behind her. His fingers dug into her hips, back arched and head fell back as he let loose inside her. Justin erupted, filling her with his seed until it flowed out of her dripping honey pot and down onto the sheets.

He lay on top of her for long moments and relished the soft stroke of Delaine's fingers over his back and shoulders. Finally her caress slowed, then stilled. She'd drifted off to sleep, but he couldn't bring himself to leave her body just yet. Carefully positioning her limp form until they lay spoon style, he reached down and pulled the covers up over them and settled down to untangle her beautiful hair with his fingers.

* * * * *

Delaine woke in the middle of the night to the feel of hard, warm male behind her. Tucked underneath a strong chin, solid thighs were pressed behind hers, a well-formed arm thrown over her hip, and her head lay on a thick biceps instead of her pillow. Goodness, she was surrounded by strong man. And she liked it.

Justin tightened his embrace, sighed in his sleep and then eased his hold. She rolled slowly away and got up to go to the bathroom. When she climbed back into bed, she lay on her side for a moment, sorting through her thoughts and everything she'd seen and heard since she'd arrived in Charlotte. In the end, all she could think about was how cold the sheets felt way over on this side of the huge bed. Then she was suddenly surrounded with warmth as Justin encircled her waist and hauled her over to his side. She snuggled close and said one simple word for the most mind-blowing sex she'd ever had in her life.

"Wow."

"Hmmm?" he sighed sleepily.

"Well, I've never had an orgasm before," she muttered sheepishly.

Justin was wide awake now and peered at her through the darkness. "What? You were married for eighteen years, had two kids and the man never made you come?"

She blushed. "Well, Gary wasn't the most attentive lover. I didn't know I could do it until you made me tonight."

Her ex-husband was obviously an idiot. She deserved so much better. Deserved someone attentive, caring. Someone like him. Before he met Delaine, he wouldn't have entertained these kinds of thoughts to save his life. Settling down wasn't something he'd planned on, especially in his line of work. But now that he'd talked with her, touched her, these kinds of permanent thoughts felt right. He didn't even question wanting to be with her. Instead, he kissed the top of her head and nuzzled the back of her neck and shoulders.

She tilted her head to give him better access to the tingly spot he'd found earlier. She took a quick intake of breath when his hand slid up from her hip to caress the underside of her breasts. It amazed her that he instinctively knew what she liked and exactly how she liked it. Reaching up to wrap her arms around his neck, her fingers brushed against something that hadn't been there when she'd fallen asleep. Gingerly she touched six neat fat braids, three on each side of her head. It was the sweetest thing anyone had ever done. Hot tears pooled behind her eyes and spilled down her cheeks until her shoulders shook with emotion.

"What is it, baby? What's wrong?" Alarm seized the inside of Justin's stomach. He held her tighter, pressing her back tight against his chest. A lump formed in his throat at her wracking sobs. He simply couldn't bear to hear her cry.

At his soft, caring words, Delaine rolled over and buried her face in his chest and bawled like a baby.

"Please, baby, tell me what's the matter. I can't stand to hear you cry," he said softly into her hair, placing soothing little kisses everywhere his lips could reach.

She hiccupped and sniffed, "You braided my hair."

"Hell, I'll take them out if it upsets you that much. I love your hair and thought you'd want it out of the way while you slept," he said as he reached up to take the braids down.

"No!" she screeched. He snatched his hands back quickly and for the first time in a long time, Justin had no idea what to do. Her next words pierced his heart.

"No one has ever combed my hair before," she sobbed. "It's such an intimate, sweet gesture, I don't know what to say. Justin, look, I don't know where this is going, or if we'll even be together next week, but thank you for making me feel so special tonight."

"You're welcome, beauty. It was my pleasure." He gently took her tear-stained face between his hands and kissed away the trail of tears. His mouth took hers in a sweet caress. Their tongues dueled lazily, but he found himself as hard and fiercely needy as the first time. Justin pulled her leg up over his hip and caressed her lovely, round ass. A finger disappeared into her pussy from behind and her hips circled against his hand. She was already wet and more than ready.

"Are you sore?" he asked, thinking if she wasn't tender from the pounding he'd given her earlier, she should be.

"Mmmm." Lord, how could he make her feel so hot and needy with so little effort? His touch made her cream, her womb clench, made her crave the finger stroking in and out of her body. He added another finger and she arched against him with a ragged moan.

"If you're sore, baby, I shouldn't make love to you again."

"Then no...not sore." Breathless, she wiggled her hips,

wanting him to sink his fingers deeper.

"Are you lying, Delaine?" He playfully nipped her ear then soothed the bite with a swipe of his tongue.

"That's my story and I'm sticking to it. Now, do you think you can make me come again? I just want to be sure I can really do it," she queried playfully, her tears a thing of the past.

"Do you think I can make you come again?" he asked, loving their word play, sliding his fingers as deep as he could get them up her creamy passage.

"Oh, yes. Yes, I definitely think so," she breathed out in a rush as his fingers were replaced with a thick, throbbing cock.

CHAPTER NINE

"Good morning, beautiful."

"Good morning, handsome," Delaine replied into her speaker phone as she ran her fingers through her thick hair to undo the twists she'd put in before she'd gone to sleep. She'd hoped he would call, and he hadn't disappointed her in the two weeks they'd been seeing each other. She was glad he couldn't see her looking at herself in her bathroom mirror, grinning like a loon.

"I enjoyed spending time with you last night," he said seductively. "When can we get together again?"

"Well, you don't waste any time getting to the point, do you?" she asked saucily.

"Baby, I don't have any time to waste. If I see a priceless jewel should I reach for it? Or should I pretend I don't see it and hope it's still there the next time I happen to come around?"

Well, didn't he have a way with words? He made her feel all warm and gooey inside, like melting caramel.

"How about dinner tonight?"

"I'm not sure if I can make it tonight," she said, disappointed that it was true. She really needed to do some surveillance. She was really close to getting what she needed on Baker but was frustrated because she wasn't further along in the case. That damned Sarah Ann was on her like white on rice since that day Delaine had shaken her off her trail.

"Have another hot date lined up already, eh," Justin said, half-serious.

"Sorry, but this sistah can't move that fast," she teased.

"Baby, I happen to like your moves," he crooned into the phone. "So how about it? My place, say, seven o'clock? If we get through dinner early, we can work on getting my bed to smell like hot sex and you, like your bed does."

"You are such a freak," she giggled.

"Yeah, and you like it."

"All right, I give!" she laughed, knowing he was out of her league when it came to sexual banter, but she was catching up. "I'll come as long as I don't have to eat delivered Chinese food."

Justin's totally male laugh made her breath catch as her insides danced at his masculine chuckle. Lord, she just loved his voice. They finalized their plans and Delaine headed out the door for what was becoming a habit of Sunday morning breakfast at Le Peep with Pam.

If Pam noticed Delaine was dressed in black tactical gear and SWAT-issued boots, she didn't mention it.

* * * * *

Justin parked several blocks away from Astin Pharma, snuck in the back gate and into the building through a back door some idiot left propped open so they could take a smoke break.

It was Saturday and there shouldn't be anyone in the building except the process engineers on the main production floors. But lately, Baker hadn't been sticking to his regular schedule. If the man was anything, he was meticulous and predictable, and Justin wondered if Delaine's presence was the reason for his out-of-character behavior.

He made his way to one of the restricted elevators,

flipped open his cell phone, hit the speed dial and spoke quietly.

"Okay, I'm in. Do your thing," he whispered into the mouthpiece. He held the display panel of the phone up to the badge scanner. A moment later a beep sounded and the elevator doors slid smoothly open. Another beep and a click later, it started its descent. Justin spoke quickly into the mouthpiece.

"Thanks, Derrick. Now tell me what you did in case I have to explain my way out of it later."

"I hacked the database and saw that Baker recently gave the Sarah Ann chick who's been tailing your girl access to The Vault. I displayed the barcode from her badge onto the screen of your digital cell. The reader in the elevator doesn't know the difference between the badge and the phone."

"But what about the logs that show who's been in and out of the elevator?"

"Baker tried to be slick by programming Sarah Ann's badge with a fictitious name, but that works to our advantage. The system won't show that either you or she were ever there."

"You're a genius. Thanks, man."

"No problem. By the way, I'm still working on getting more details on Delaine. We're almost one hundred percent sure she's with Aegis, which is good for us. Spencer's calling one of his contacts to verify. And there's a small problem."

"What?" Justin asked impatiently, not liking the hesitation in his partner's voice.

"You're going to have to keep an even closer eye on Delaine than you already are."

Justin's brow furrowed as a lump formed in the pit of his stomach. This couldn't possibly be good. Hell, he'd been spending so much time with Delaine, if he watched her any closer he'd be living with her. While that particular thought held appeal, he pushed it away and focused on the conversation with Derrick.

"What do you mean keep a closer eye on her?"

"Because Baker knows she's undercover. I don't know how, but she's been compromised."

This was not what he wanted to hear. Baker was a dangerous son of a bitch and the thought of anything happening to Delaine at his hands made the blood behind Justin's eyes boil. He was so angry, he literally saw red. "Shit!" Justin fumed, raking his hand through his thick red hair as the elevator continued to plummet.

"My sentiments exactly. All indications are the two of you are on the same side. Why don't you just talk to her about what we know?"

"Are you crazy? And have Spencer fry my ass?" Justin growled into the mouthpiece, squeezing the phone so hard it was a wonder the thing didn't break in two.

"Look, Justin, you've never been this crazy about a woman in the ten years I've been working with you. I know you care about her. Besides, Baker is your target, not Delaine. I'm not saying you should blow your own cover, but talking to her about Baker may be the only way she'll let you help her. I know you can come up with some way to talk to her about Baker without telling her you're D.E.A."

"Look, Derrick, there's no way in hell I'm lying to Delaine! I'll just have to watch her back without her finding out."

"You don't have authorization for that, man. You know regulations."

"Fuck regulations! She's my woman, damn it! And I'm not going to let Baker get his hands on her just because the regs say I can't get involved in another agent's case without auth!"

"All right, man, I feel you. I'll run it by Spencer and get back to you."

"What the hell do I do in the meantime?"

"If Delaine hears from someone else that you're

working the same case, she's going to fry your ass and you won't have to worry about Spencer. She's a sistah, and they don't play. Trust me, I know. And there's the possibility that if Baker knows …

"…then someone else knows too," Justin reasoned quickly. "Damn it! I may have no choice but to talk to her, but not today. I'll catch up with you later, Derrick. I'm going to lose the signal any second. Almost at the bottom."

"Good luck, man."

"Yeah, thanks." Justin disconnected the call and turned off his cell completely. He flipped it over to make sure the homing beacon still flashed faintly, then slipped it into his back pocket just as the elevator doors hissed open.

* * * * *

Delaine walked right through the front door, her long cloak hiding the jacket and black tactical gear. She headed straight for her office, locked the door and did a little creative hacking. In minutes she'd bypassed the main security camera program and fed the digital photos she wanted the security guards to see into the system that controlled all the camera links. The program would only run for ten minutes, which was more than enough time to get into a restricted elevator unseen.

Her badge and digital key worked perfectly, just like before, and in moments she was speeding down to The Vault. Before the doors opened, she checked the guns in the holsters under her jacket, a lethal black bowie knife tucked in her boot and the homing device hidden behind her ear.

She knew exactly which lab she needed to break into, having explored all the tunnels over the last few weeks. Every tunnel led to a legitimate research and development lab, except for the two tunnels on the far right. Both these labs were always locked. The first, which she'd successfully broken into, appeared to be scrubbed clean after every use. Whoever had been using it left no evidence of what they were doing in there. She'd found no dust, no residue. Not even a fingerprint. The second tunnel led to an identical lab she hadn't been in yet. It was larger and had another door near the back. And she headed straight to it.

She encountered no one as she slipped her gloves on and picked the lock. Once inside, she eased the door closed and slid the deadbolt home. A quick sweep of this front room found it clean but not spotless. There were a couple of used vials, a pair of tweezers and even a small dissolution test kit. On one of the metal tables she found a small bit of some kind of pink powder. Delaine put a sample in a small glass vial, careful not to inhale or get it anywhere on her skin or clothes. Sealed and secured in a plastic baggie, she tucked it inside her inner jacket pocket and made her way to the door at the back of the room.

Closing the door softly behind her, she threw the deadbolt and stepped fully into the room. Her gut promptly twisted. This room was soundproof and would prevent her from hearing anyone approach. She'd have to work fast. She passed by the lab equipment, three doors that she assumed were closets for storage, along with file cabinets, and went directly to a wide-screen monitor with playback equipment hooked up to it. The playback cables were connected to three video cameras arranged in front of small neatly made beds, and a medical table with stirrups on one end.

Delaine went to the digital video camera. There was still a tape inside. She popped it into the playback unit and Baker's face immediately came up on the screen. The date and time at the bottom of the screen was six-thirty yesterday morning.

Baker moved away from the screen and a blonde woman Delaine had seen a couple of times in the lunchroom sat on one of the beds naked. Her arms were crossed over her breasts, her legs clenched tightly and her head down. She looked up at Baker through lowered lashes and appeared decidedly uncomfortable. But this blonde wasn't the one she'd seen in her vision.

In the video, he approached the woman with a little pink tablet balanced on the end of his finger. Delaine's hand immediately felt for the vial inside her jacket, wondering if the residue inside was from the same stuff. Baker placed the tablet under the girl's tongue and the timer on the video started counting.

At thirty seconds, the girl still sat on the edge of the bed, but her eyes were now wide and frightened. Her hands dropped to her breasts and she watched her hands massage and pull on them as if she couldn't believe what she was doing to herself.

At a full minute, the woman writhed on the bed, pumping her hips at something that wasn't there. Her legs fell open and she ground down into the mattress. As she panted and moaned, her eyes followed Baker's every movement.

At two minutes, she wept and begged Baker to take her. The perverted bastard obliged.

Delaine watched the tape and almost gagged when he approached the bed with his skinny hard cock poking out of the fly of his pants. He lay down on top of the woman and her legs immediately wrapped around his hips. The woman was like a wild animal under him and screamed, yelled and clawed at his back while he pumped into her body with his pants, shoes and shirt still on. The woman came on a tormented scream. Then Baker flipped her over, told her to get up on her hands and knees and took her from behind. She screamed as she came again.

No wonder the walls were soundproof. Baker had plowed his blonde guinea pig for fifteen minutes and she'd come several times. When he was done, she still writhed and rolled around on the bed. Then Sarah Ann came into the picture. Before the blonde collapsed from exhaustion, she'd come almost non-stop, compliments of Sarah Ann and a dildo.

Sapa roared loud and long in her mind. The lioness had

obviously been trying to warn her about something, but she'd been so absorbed in the disgusting video, she hadn't been paying attention. Delaine snapped out of her incredulity at the turn of a key in the lock. Shit! She snatched the tape out of the playback unit, stuffed it into her pocket and moved silently to the first closet door. Hell, it was locked and there was no way she'd have time to pick it. On to the second door. Locked. Relief coursed through her when the third door opened and closed smoothly just before Baker stepped into the room.

'Sapa, I need a little help with my hearing,' Delaine called to her spirit guide. The great hunter's keen senses flowed through the bond and manifested inside Delaine's body. Through the door, she heard everything going on in the lab as if she were sitting right there. Crouched in the dark, she listened while Baker fussed at Sarah Ann for dead-bolting the doors and leaving the lights on.

Ready to take the bastard down, she silently unsnapped the secure strap on her holster to slide her gun free. Delaine had all the proof she needed.

A wicked, sharp knife pressed against her throat from behind. She didn't move a hair further.

CHAPTER TEN

Justin couldn't believe it. The woman was supposed to be having breakfast with Pam, not nearly getting herself killed. He was furious.

"Don't make a sound, Delaine, or we're both dead," he hissed as he removed the blade from her throat and pocketed it in the sheath hidden in his boot.

She hissed to her spirit guide, 'Damn it, Sapa. Why didn't you warn me Justin was here?'

Because he is not a danger to us.

He pressed so tightly against her back, she was practically in his lap. Against her will, her skin heated and her nipples tingled. She didn't need this, not right now. She needed to concentrate on taking down the bad guy.

"What the hell are you doing here, Justin?" she whispered furiously to her man crouched behind her.

"Can we talk about this later and concentrate on getting out of here in one piece?"

"I'm a law enforcement officer. Don't interfere with the arrest I'm about to make," she warned in a no-nonsense tone.

"Don't think so, baby. Baker is alone in this room, but he's not alone in the facility. If we're discovered, we'll find ourselves 'disappeared', and probably with lots of pain involved."

She cocked her head to the side. "Baker has allies here? In the building?" She clearly wondered how much he knew that she didn't.

"Justin, who…"

"Later, Delaine."

"No, now. All we can do is wait until Baker leaves. I think we've got time."

Her tone was snide. He was so pissed, he didn't care. "I'm not willing to wait that long," Justin snapped quietly then flipped open his cell phone and turned it on. He breathed a sigh of relief while grumbling about poor signals in a state-of-the-art facility.

He whispered into the mouthpiece. "Hey, Derrick, it's me. We're stuck in Baker's lab. Confirm the passage behind door number three." After a couple of seconds, he said, "Excellent." He clicked the phone shut and listened. It sounded like Baker was having hot and sweaty sex with Sarah Ann. Good.

"Sounds like the perfect time to get the hell out of here. Stand up, and step where I step." He pressed a button on the back of his cell phone and a thin beam of blue light appeared, just bright enough to see the floor of the little room.

She followed silently, her back stiff with anger and her brows drawn so tightly together she felt the beginning of a fierce headache. Delaine couldn't remember being this angry since the jacked-up e-mail from Gary a year ago. It had been a long time since she'd been this frightened for someone she cared about. And she didn't like it one bit. She was royally pissed. If she said a single word, it would be a very long, loud mistake.

* * * * *

With Derrick's guidance, it took Justin less than a minute to find and open a small hidden hatch set into the wall at the back of the closet. It was one of many that had been used to get building materials down to The Vault when it was being secretly built. Once through it, he turned off the small flashlight built into his phone and they moved silently up a narrow hallway until they reached a steep stairwell. It took them another twenty minutes to climb up to the first floor. They emerged outside at the rear of the building covered with dust and cobwebs, their lungs burning from their adrenaline-fueled jaunt up those endless steps. By the time they reached the rear parking lot, they were both huffing, puffing and sneezing all over the place.

Justin packed Delaine into his car and sped her home. He clenched his jaw to keep silent, not trusting himself to speak to her just now. He knew his reaction to discovering her down in the The Vault ready to draw on Baker was unreasonable. She was, after all, an undercover agent like himself. It was her job to find evidence on people like him and take them down. But the thought of her charging out of their hiding place to confront Baker scared the red out of his hair. Delaine in any kind of danger set his teeth on edge. He gripped the steering wheel of his Jag until his knuckles turned white.

He pulled into her driveway and she slammed out of the car before he could get the emergency brake in place. She stomped through the front door, stripped off her soiled, filthy clothes in the foyer and sprinted up the stairs.

Justin got an eyeful of a very naked Delaine, cobweb-filled hair flying behind her as she took the stairs two at a time. He stopped short and stared after her. His anger faded as his body tensed with baser emotions. Damn, she had such a nice ass. Would he ever get used to his physical reaction to this woman? Not bloody likely.

He stripped off his dirty clothes, piled them on top of Delaine's and took the whole pile to the laundry room before following her up the stairs.

* * * * *

Fuming, Delaine jumped into the gigantic glass brick

shower in her bedroom and slammed the door behind her. How dare that man put himself in such danger! She was so mad, she couldn't think straight. He looked more than capable of taking care of himself, but didn't he know how dangerous it was snooping around in The Vault? And he had to be snooping, otherwise he wouldn't have been crouching in that stupid closet. The big question was, who the hell did he snoop for? As a contractor, he could end up working at some other pharma company next week. Perhaps he planned to take Astin trade secrets with him? *'Oh please don't let him be a bad guy.'* She already had one crook to catch, and the last thing she needed was to fall for one. And what if he got hurt in the meantime? What a mess.

One thought led to another, and by the time she angled one of the large shower heads to rush over her body, leaned back against the cool glass brick wall, the bath seat solid under thighs, she was a volatile mix of confusion and fury. Forcing herself to relax, she breathed deeply as the hot water splashed over her head and down her tired, aching body like a warm, gentle waterfall. The steam-covered door swung silently open and a cool whoosh of air washed over her. Justin.

Again, Sapa hadn't warned of his approach. What was up with that?

She opened her eyes and pushed her thick cottony locks back and away from her face. The soothing scents of rosemary, lavender and peppermint filled the air just as his big hands sank into her curls to lather her hair with her favorite shampoo. His fingers moved expertly through the mass of coils until every inch of her scalp tingled.

"How in the world do you know so much about hair? Black hair at that?" she breathed contentedly. It felt so good, and his strokes were so gentle, working from her roots clear to the ends of her hair. She leaned into his hands and sighed softly with pleasure. He stepped to the side and the waterfall of water flowed down over her body again, rinsing her hair clean.

"Three younger sisters." He kept his reply soft and controlled.

"It feels wonderful," Delaine murmured. How could she stay mad at a man who shampooed her hair? Lather was worked through her hair again and rinsed until all traces of shampoo flowed down the drain and her body threatened to slide off the bath seat along with the puddle of suds.

She started to tell him if she didn't hurry up and moisturize the mop on her head, it would be good and nappy. Instead, she snapped her mouth closed at his attentiveness. One step ahead of her, he was already smoothing a handful of creamy conditioner through her tresses and massaging it through. But now that she thought about it, he always seemed to be one step ahead of her. How?

Suddenly her body cooled and ached at the loss of contact. Justin had stepped away. Her eyes snapped opened and his blazing blue gaze trapped her with its intensity. He held out his hand to her.

"Come here, baby."

Delaine quirked a brow and wondered at the tone in his voice. His jaw ticked furiously, but she did as he asked, stood slowly and stepped into his arms.

He held her close, trembling as he said, "Delaine, I was furious today. The thought of anything happening to you made me crazy." His voice tight with emotion as his hands stroked up and down her back. "I don't think I've been that angry since…hell, I've never been that angry."

"Then you've read my mind," she whispered back. "I know you work for Astin, but The Vault just isn't a safe place to be found right now. I checked the list of authorized personnel and your name wasn't on it, Justin. What the hell were you doing down there?"

"I don't want to talk about that right now. I'm so relieved you're safe, I just want to hold you and never let go. I need to feel you, Del. Let me touch you, baby."

He sat her back down on the bath seat and knelt between her legs. Even on his knees, they were still of a height. He rubbed his nose against hers and whispered all the nasty things he wanted to do to her.

"Baby, I want to nibble and suck on your pretty tits and lick you from the underside to the nipples until you squirm. Then I want to kiss a path from between your beautiful breasts, down to your navel and back up again before I take them in my hands, squeeze them together and slide my dick back and forth between them."

Delaine wanted him to do that and more. His erotic words stoked the low simmer in her womb to a full-blown forest fire.

"I want to suck on the lobes of your ears then slip my tongue up around them. Work my way slowly down your neck to that spot near your shoulder that makes you scream."

"Oh, yes," she hissed through her teeth while her hips moved in a slow restless rhythm as Justin knelt between her legs. One hand massaged the sensitive nipple of one breast while the other found her swollen clit peeking out of its little hood so he could play with it.

He slipped a finger into her mouth and said, "I love how you suck my finger. Your mouth is so hot and wet."

Delaine had never enjoyed oral sex, but suddenly she wanted it with this man. Wanted it almost more than she wanted to feel him moving inside her, more than she needed to breathe.

She stood and pushed him from his knees down to the shower floor. The scent of his body mingled with the steam of the shower into an intoxicating perfume that tickled her nose and made her pussy weep. The second he lay back on the warm, wet tiles she plunged her mouth down over his engorged length with an urgency that took his breath away. He bit his lip, holding back a primal yell when she began sucking his flesh like she wanted nothing more in the world than to take him all the way down her throat and milk him dry.

Her firm lips wrapped tightly around his shaft, swallowing as much of him as she could. Her free hand pumped him eagerly as she pulled her mouth up to the engorged head and swirled her tongue around and around the purple tip before plunging back down.

When she hummed her pleasure the vibration crashed down his sensitive nerve endings to pool at the base of his sac. He almost came on the spot. He sat up swiftly, lifted her high and slid deep in one lightning quick stroke.

"Oh yes! Oh, Justin! Oh, god!" she babbled, an overloaded bundle of nerves but full of a need so beyond the physical, she was humbled by it.

"More!"

"Demanding woman, aren't you?" Justin teased, his jaw clenched tightly as he listened to her demand that he take her harder, give her more, make her scream. Determined to keep his woman happy, he gave her just what she asked for.

He plumbed deep and almost died of the exquisite pleasure of being surrounded by her tight, gripping sheath. His blood churned thick and hot through his veins as he struggled to think clearly through the haze of bliss that was Delaine. He savored the feel of her strong hands as they touched him everywhere she could reach, blazing a trail up his chest and over his neck to fist in his hair. She yanked and pulled as she rode him.

Up off her knees in a move that surprised him, Delaine put her feet flat on the floor and squatted over him. Nothing touched him but her sweet, shaved core. She rode him like his dick had the antidote to her need loaded inside. He reached between their bodies and found her little swollen knot. His fingers pulled and stroked, drove her higher until the walls of her tight sheath squeezed him unmercifully.

She cried out when Justin lifted her off of him. She

yelled for him to put her back. Put her back right now, damn it. Instead, he positioned her on her knees, chest against the bath seat, and plunged deep from behind. Now, she really did cry. The tears flowed down the wet skin of her cheeks as she pleaded for him to fulfill her need. She begged. Demanded. Screamed. And still he rocked into her, his balls slapping against her ass, only to slow down just enough to keep her release at bay.

"Justin, I can't take anymore!" she yelled. "If you don't...oh god...finish me, I'll castrate. Your ass! Over! Breakfast!"

"Ah, baby, you feel so good!" Justin growled in response. "I could fuck you forever. This is my pussy. All mine."

"Yes, Justin. Take it, take it now."

"You sure this is mine, my pussy?" he panted into her hair.

"Yesssssss!"

He pistoned into her, the veins of his thick staff stimulating her beyond reason. She felt her orgasm begin down in her toes, streak up her thighs and circle around her hips. Then it dove straight down and she erupted like a sunburst where their bodies were joined.

Justin filled her completely, pushing himself to the place only he could reach until he was submerged in her. Delaine reached back between her legs and pressed against the sensitive spot underneath his balls. It was over. His head flew back on a loud cry as his seed geysered against her womb, triggering another round of shuddering deep inside her thirsty heat.

They basked in the afterglow of their lovemaking until the water ran cold. Finally remembering Delaine still had conditioner in her hair, he washed it out for her before they washed each other quickly and headed for the big bed to fall into an exhausted stupor. But not before Justin admitted to himself that he was in deep. And he had no desire to be anywhere else.

In the morning he would tell Delaine who he was and exactly what he was doing at Astin Pharma, consequences be damned.

* * * * *

Oh hell, it was almost time to meet Pam for breakfast again. After the night with Justin, she wasn't sure she was up to it. She rolled over and bumped into his broad, muscular back. Not only had the gorgeous hunk saved her neck, but he'd laid some sex down on her like she'd never had it before. And she'd be damned if he didn't have the sexiest ass she'd ever seen on a man. Sigh. She hadn't found out what he was doing down in The Vault, but since he hadn't killed or exposed her, she could only assume he worked there. But for who?

"Hey, you," she whispered sleepily, shaking Justin's shoulder on a yawn. It was like trying to shake a mountain. She ran her fingers through his red bed-head and crooned against the back of his neck. "Get up, honey, I need to get going."

Justin groaned, rolled over and smashed the pillow down over his head. She poked him in the ribs in the only spot on his hard body she'd found to be ticklish. He flinched and was out of the bed in two snaps, taking half the covers with him. She watched his eyes drop to her washboard stomach then slide lower to the smooth triangle between her legs. The predator was back with a wicked gleam in his eye and a cock rising to attention before her very eyes.

Oh damn! Delaine jumped out of the bed, snatched a pair of jeans and a tee shirt off the chest at the foot of the bed and fled the room, calling over her shoulder, "I'm meeting Pam in an hour. I'll shower in the guest bathroom, 'cause if I shower with you I'll never get out of here."

He taunted her fleeing back, "Damn straight! Come back here and take it like a man, er, wo-man!"

A buck naked Delaine ran down the stairs and headed to one of the guest bathrooms. Afterward, she went into the kitchen and put the kettle on for tea. She stood near the phone, nibbling on a fingernail, contemplating. Finally picking it up, her nails tap, tap, tapped against the gray granite countertop as she waited for the line to pick up on the other side.

"This is Geri."

"Hey, boss. I'm sending you a package. I got the goods on Baker!"

"Yeah! I knew you could do it. You are, after all, one of the best."

"Flattery will get you everywhere, madam boss."

"So whatcha got?"

"The most foul digital video of Baker doing some interesting things in The Vault. I managed to filch some samples too. They'll need to be analyzed to find out exactly what he's making, but I think it's some kind of synthetic aphrodisiac."

"Are you ready to wrap this up?"

"Not quite. All I need to do is catch him in The Vault, and he's as good as done. By the way, did you get the info on Justin Cooley back yet?"

"It came in last night. Hold on a minute, let me pull it up."

Delaine was anxious and felt more than a little guilty about checking him out behind his back. She kept telling herself that it was just part of the job, but her heart wasn't buying it. And neither did Sapa, who'd been quiet since last night but was now growling her disapproval in the back of Delaine's mind. The one minute she stood on hold seemed to stretch on forever while she listened to the click of Geri's fingers on her computer keyboard.

"Okay, Delaine, some of this info is dated. Let's see, former Marine, black ops, honorable discharge… Here we go, he's D.E.A. Distinguished record with the department for ten years. Hold on, let me check something else."

D.E.A.? Drug Enforcement Administration? Damn it! After their little closet rendevous in The Vault, Delaine was sure he was a thief with a few high tech toys, not a fucking agent!

Delaine heard Geri pick up another line and ask to speak to someone whose name she couldn't quite make out. She distinctly heard the name Cooley, and a few uh-huhs before her boss came back to the phone.

"Delaine?"

"I'm here."

"He's part of Spencer's team."

"Spencer!" Damn, that meant he wasn't just D.E.A., but more like a super covert "Bond. James Bond" type of D.E.A. guy. Shit! This just got better and better. "Geri, since when does D.E.A. encroach on another agents case? How the hell did I not know there was D.E.A. in my goddamned face?" She felt like a complete idiot.

"Actually, it's our fault. Somehow we missed some intelligence somewhere…" Geri began.

"Yeah, sure it's our fault. We missed something. More like I missed something. Goddamned, son-of-a-bitch, just wait until I get my hands…" Delaine growled in a low voice.

"Delaine, what's wrong?"

"I'll call you back, Geri," she said softly and disconnected the line. She picked it up and dialed again.

"Pam? Hey, it's me. I can't make it today. Something's come up with work. Let's try it next week, all right?"

* * * * *

Justin stepped out of the shower, walked out of the bathroom and came face-to-face with a royally pissed off Delaine.

"You're D.E.A.!"

Damn! Knowing he couldn't lie to her, he simply nodded his head and watched a mix of emotions, including rage and sadness, fly across her beautiful face.

Delaine's heart sank. The bastard had used her. She felt Sapa reach through the bond, trying to calm her.

Suta Winyan, do not push away our mate unnecessarily.

Delaine pushed the awareness of the black lioness away. Sapa retreated, with no choice but to wait until Delaine reached out to her. Unless there was danger, the spirit guide could not override her charge's wishes.

"Why did it take a call from my boss to find out who you are?"

"Delaine, I've wanted to tell you, but I couldn't. You know how this business works. You don't expose a cover to anyone without clearance. Besides, baby, when I'm with you the last thing I want to think or talk about is work. I swear I'd made up my mind to tell you, then yesterday with you in The Vault…it scared me, baby, and all I could think about was holding you."

He stepped to her with the need to wrap his arms around her and dip his nose into the hollow of her neck where she always smelled so good. But more than anything, he needed her to trust him. Justin blew out an exasperated breath as she shoved him back, or tried to.

"Nice try," she snapped. "You didn't tell me because you wanted to get the drop on Baker."

"Delaine, don't be ridiculous. After that near disaster yesterday, I planned to tell you everything this morning anyway."

"Sure you did. You can say anything now that you're fucking busted!" She walked back and forth across the carpet with her fist jammed into her hip. "How could I have been so stupid? You wanted a little booty and all of the credit for the bust. That's what I get for falling for…"

Justin shook his head in wonder. Would he ever understand the female mind? He'd saved her life, treated her like a queen, and she was upset because he didn't want to tell her he was undercover? He just couldn't comprehend it. Especially since she'd had no intention of telling him she was undercover herself. It was insane.

But insane or not, he wanted her. Needed her. Hell, he'd even admit falling in love with her, but not in her present mood. He dropped his head on a sigh. Hopefully she'd come to her senses quickly and not do anything stupid in the meantime. Like go after Baker alone. The last thing he wanted was for her to get hurt trying to hurry up and wrap this case before all the ends were tied up. He had one more card to play.

"Delaine, your cover was compromised. I was trying to keep you out of trouble."

"I didn't need you to keep me out of trouble."

"Damn it, you stubborn woman, did you hear what I said? You were compromised!"

"I could have handled it on my own. So tell me the truth, Justin. What were you really after, huh? You've been in this business for a long time. Ready to retire? Needed to go out with a bang?"

"Damn it, Delaine, I told you what I was after. Yes, I was originally sent here to find out if Baker was secretly developing an illegal substance. But after I found out you were involved and in danger I couldn't just leave you for the dogs. Not after getting to know you, baby."

"Riiiight," she drawled sarcastically.

"Look, I won't stand here and be accused of lying," he growled dangerously, his own anger starting to kindle.

"Good! Then get dressed and get the hell out!" Delaine pointed toward the door.

"Fine!" Justin grabbed his clothes off the end of the bed, stepped into his pants and yanked his shirt over his head, wet hair and all. Not bothering with underwear, socks or shoes, he slammed down the stairs and out the front door. The wheels of his Jag echoed in the quiet morning air as he squealed out of the driveway and tore down the street.

CHAPTER ELEVEN

Delaine's stomach dropped into her shoes every time her phone rang. For the past three days, she'd taken to letting her voice mail get it, but every time she checked her messages it was never the one person she wanted it to be—Justin. She continued to show up for work at Astin and perform her job expertly as if nothing had gone down. Close to getting a sign-off on her hierarchy design, she knew she was running out of time to wrap this case. Geri told her where Justin was supposed to be working inside the Astin facility, but as the days passed with no sight or sign of him, Delaine's ability to rethink the matter finally resurfaced.

She admitted to herself that she was miserable, hated that the two of them had fought. Hated sleeping without him pressed up against her. Her days weren't as bright. Her smile felt brittle, as if the facade she'd perfected was crumbling. Even Sapa was irritated. Her spirit guide came when called, but the warmth that usually flowed through the bond had noticeably cooled. The great huntress sulked behind Delaine's eyes with drooping ears and her grey cat eyes full of sadness.

Perhaps she had behaved foolishly? After all, she'd had

no intention of telling Justin she worked for Aegis. So why was she upset that he hadn't confided that he was D.E.A.? Her boss was even willing to take heat since Aegis actually dropped the ball. While uncommon, it wasn't unheard of for intelligence to miss a few key details. It was a huge blunder but nothing that couldn't be fixed. And since they were on the same side, was there really anything to be upset about? Sapa stirred restlessly.

Suta Winyan, you are being unfair. If you would but think instead of react you would discover your true feelings.

She thought on Sapa's words and felt somewhat silly. Cutting Justin off cold like that, she'd cut off her nose to spite her face.

You are sabotaging our chance for a worthy mate. You are running away.

'Oh, hush already.' Delaine scowled into the recesses of her mind, knowing the black lioness was right. But she didn't want to talk to the big cat about her catapulting emotions. She wanted to talk to a flesh and blood woman. She called Geri.

"Delaine, why are you being such a brick head? Justin is a really good guy. I called Spencer directly to check it out. He told me that as soon as Justin learned from his partner that your cover was blown, he sought permission to cover your ass. He didn't have to do that, you know."

Damn, it had been easier when she thought he was a bastard. Then she could have at least felt less foolish for flipping out on him.

"So who compromised me, Geri?"

"We think it was your tail in R&D. Your paperwork went through Purchasing instead of Human Resources. Some idiot put a code on the requisition used only for the FDA or other law enforcement agencies. Sarah Ann had been dating the main procurement officer in Purchasing. Spencer thinks she saw the code and alerted Baker."

"That would explain why she's been on me since day one."

"Yep, and Justin could have let you crash and burn and continued with his own investigation. It would have been perfectly ethical."

"Thanks, Geri. Gotta run," Delaine said calmly while her guilt ate her alive.

"Hold on a minute. Spencer and I want you two to close this case out together. We think it's safer."

"But the case is blown," Delaine said firmly, hating the words as she spoke them. She'd never failed an assignment in her five years at Aegis, or all her eighteen years undercover.

"The case isn't blown. Baker is not aware of Justin's involvement at all. You just continue to paint yourself as the agent who doesn't know she's been exposed and use it to urge Baker to act. To do something stupid."

"Done. I'll contact Justin and talk to you later."

Delaine hung up and dialed Justin's cell phone. It was three in the morning and wasn't surprised when she got his voice mail. She left a message for him to meet her for breakfast after she got a few hours sleep. Then she hung up and called his home phone just in case.

Big mistake.

* * * * *

"Hu-woe?" a female voice drawled on the other end of the line.

"Hello? Who is this? Pam?"

"Yeah, wha'is it?"

"What do you mean, what is it? What are you doing at Justin's house? And at three in the morning?"

"I'm sthpending the night," Pam slurred and almost dropped the phone from her boneless fingers.

"What!"

"I sorry, girl. I just couldn't help m'self. Don't be mad, 'kay?"

"Don't be mad? You're sleeping with my man and you're telling me don't be mad?"

"Your man? I thought you din't wan him an-more, Del.

I mean, you kicked him to da curb, so finers, keepers, girl," she slurred. Pam hung up and smiled when the phone didn't ring again.

Justin appeared in the doorway of his bedroom in a pair of comfy terry sweats. He padded across the living room in bare feet, a towel around his neck to catch the water dripping from his hair. His blue eyes darkened and flashed his annoyance with his unexpected houseguest.

"Who was that on the phone, Pam?" he asked impatiently.

Pam looked up from her temporary bed on the couch and yawned widely. "Naa sure," she lied, her words running together almost incoherently. "I heeerd dit ringed, but I dinn't cath it afore dey hanged up."

"Good, because you don't have any business answering my phone. I'm done in the shower. If you want to take one, hurry up. I just picked up a message on my cell to meet Delaine for breakfast first thing in the morning, so I want to get to bed."

"Thure thing, han-some," she smiled cattily as she rose on unsteady, rubber band legs.

Justin wrinkled his nose when she let all the blankets fall to the floor to reveal her slim, naked flesh. She had a nice enough body, but he'd never been less interested in a woman as he was tonight. The smell of alcohol permeated her pores, disgusting him as she shimmied up to him and ran her hands across his bare chest.

"I—uh, I really 'preciate you lettin' me crash here, Jus. If there's a way I can, uh, repay you, I'm more sthan game."

He shivered, but not from lust. It was a good thing he'd eaten dinner hours ago. Her touch made him want to blow chunks. And this was supposed to be Delaine's good friend? He removed her hands from his chest and spoke through gritted teeth.

"Look, bitch, hit the couch or hit the road. You have ten minutes to get your ass to bed or get out of here. I belong to Delaine, heart and soul."

"Bud you two hadda fight. She duzznt want you."

"It doesn't matter. I want her. And it's a good thing I don't hit women, or I'd beat your ass for betraying her like this."

He turned on a bare heel, stalked into his room and slammed the door shut.

CHAPTER TWELVE

Delaine took the long way to the restaurant then drove on by. She just couldn't face Justin today. She'd left a message asking him to meet her here, but after that conversation with Pam there really wasn't anything else to say. He'd obviously moved on. If Justin wanted Pam, fine, he could have her. But what started raggedy would end up raggedy. And those two raggedy mogillas deserved each other.

Her heart was in a million pieces, but she refused to feel the hurt anymore. Instead, she focused on her anger and let it consume her until she shook with rage. Bastard! And Pam? She couldn't believe Pam would steal her man like that. She'd sat up in that girl's chair at the salon and told her all of her and Justin's business, so it's not like the woman didn't know Delaine was serious about him. For someone she'd known since their children were in preschool to stab her in the back like this was beyond painful. Oh lord, what was she going to do?

Suta, you are not using wisdom. This man is not like the puny Gary person.

'But he slept with my best friend, Sapa! Hell, at least Gary slept with someone I didn't know.' She slammed her

117

hand down on the steering wheel then looked down, expecting to see blood on her shirt from her breaking heart.

Your reasoning abilities are unsurpassed. Use them now. All is not as it appears, Suta. Trust me.

'I do trust you, Sapa. I just don't trust anyone else,' she replied sadly as a lone tear made its way down her cheek.

Fifteen minutes after she was supposed to meet him, his cell phone number popped up on the caller id. She pressed the ignore button, turned the phone off and threw it in the passenger seat. Heartsick but determined not to cry over a man ever again, she dashed the tears away and instead did something she hadn't done in all the years she'd worked with Aegis. She called in sick.

She flew home, stuffed a weekend bag with clothes, books and nothing related to work, jumped back in her Jag and headed for Nantahala Gorge. A nice quiet cabin in the Blue Ridge Mountains was just what she needed.

* * * * *

Justin hadn't called Delaine since she'd gone mental on him at finding out he was D.E.A. But it was only to give her time to cool off. He'd been totally surprised to get her message asking him to meet her for breakfast.

He'd dialed her cell several times, but it just rang and rang. Now it was going straight to voice mail. This didn't make any sense. The woman had called him and left a message saying she wanted to see him then didn't show up? He drove over to her house and rang the bell. At first he thought she just wasn't answering the door, but after walking all the way around the house, noting the closed blinds on every window, he peeked through the small glass on the door that led into the garage from the side of the house. Her car was gone. Damn, she wasn't home.

His shoulders tensed and he felt the beginnings of a nasty headache creep up the back of his neck. Flipping open his cell, he dialed her again. Where the hell was his damned woman? Had something happened that made it impossible for her to meet him? What if she'd run into trouble related to her case? What if she was casing Astin and got caught? And why the hell wasn't she answering her phone?!

He drove toward home, his chest tight with one part anger for the way she'd arbitrarily dismissed him and one part worry at not knowing if she was all right. It wasn't unheard of for someone to die in their particular line of work. Tired of leaving the stubborn woman messages, he finally called Derrick.

"Hey, Derrick. What's up?"

"The usual. Chasing bad guys and doing favors for you."

"Then everything is normal, isn't it?" Justin said glibly.

"What the hell's wrong with you, Jus?" Derrick asked with a bit of a grin in his voice.

"I need to know where Delaine is. She's not answering her cell phone, she's not at home and I haven't seen her since we fell out a few days ago. She called me in the middle of the night and asked me to meet her for breakfast then she didn't show up. She's got the goods on Baker. I need to know she's safe."

"And what if she's safe but avoiding you?"

Justin took a deep breath and his head conjured an image of Derrick, his mouth drawn tight with disapproval. The man had a way of making him feel like the little brother right after the big brother said, "I'm gonna tell dad on you". He steeled himself and got ready for the I-told-you-so. "Delaine found out I was D.E.A. And not from me."

"Man, didn't I tell you to talk to her? I told you sistahs don't play that junk," Derrick said, managing to sound stern and sorry for Justin at the same time.

But there wasn't anything he could do about it now, except try to patch things up with the woman he knew he had to be with at all costs. Whatever it took. He wasn't even shocked anymore at how strong his feelings were for

Delaine. He knew he had to find her.

"Look, Derrick, you were right, okay. But right now, I need to know my woman is all right."

"Let me work on it. I'll call you back in half an hour."

"Thanks, man."

"No problem. By the way, Spencer spoke to her boss, which is probably why she called last night. You two are supposed to close this case out together. If you can get her to speak to you ever again, that is."

* * * * *

Delaine sat on the back porch of her little cabin and meditated. It was so peaceful and quiet here. No TV. No phone. Not even a decent cell phone signal. Only the rushing of the Nantahala River through the sheer cliffs of the gorge in the distance, and a light wind whispering through the thick towering trees. She'd never seen so many huge trees in her life. They were bare, preparing for the coming winter, but it was still beautiful up here. She shivered, wrapping the extra blankets she'd found in one of the closets more closely around her body.

'What possessed me to literally run for the hills with the thick of winter approaching?' she asked herself.

Stop running, Suta. Embrace our mate. He comes.

'Yeah, whatever,' Delaine words were flat and uncaring, and in truth, she hadn't really been listening to what Sapa was saying to her along the bond.

The sleek mountain cat rolled her eyes and stalked away to a quiet corner of Delaine's mind. Before she retreated, Delaine felt her frustration. Well, she could forget about meditating. All she could think about was Justin. Justin's lips. Justin's hands on her body. Justin treating her like the queen he proclaimed her to be. Cooking for her. Taking her on road trips.

Justin sleeping with her best friend. Rather, a chick that was supposed to be her friend.

She wanted to knock herself in the head. What had she been thinking to get involved with him anyway? He was too nice, too perfect. And you know what they say—if it looks too good to be true, it probably is. So here she was again, in a relationship with a man who couldn't keep his dick out of another woman's pants. Her boss might think he was a good guy, but Delaine saw him as nothing but Gary-Number-Two.

Grumbling under her breath, she rose from the back porch and stomped into the cabin. She hit the sheets early, determined not to lose any more sleep over Justin, Pam or her job.

Bam! Bam! Bam!

What the hell was that? On silent feet, Delaine jumped out of bed with her gun in hand. She checked the lock on the window in her bedroom then edged her way to the small living room.

Bam! Bam! Bam!

Someone was banging on the door like they were the police. That was fine, because if it wasn't the police, whoever it was would limp away with a bullet in the ass.

"Delaine! Open the door!"

She lowered her weapon and clicked on the safety. Justin? Oh my god. How the hell had he found her? Okay, now that was a stupid question, she thought, shaking her head. The man worked for one of the most sophisticated covert organizations in the country. Of course he could find her.

Geesh, Delaine, get yourself together, girl, she grumbled at herself. 'And Sapa, stop all that pacing. It's making me dizzy.' An irritated growl resonated along the bond.

Sapa had told her Justin would come for her. She hadn't believed it one whit, not while he had someone else's warm body to bury his cock in. But Sapa had been wrong, in a manner of speaking. He hadn't come for her. The bastard had come for Pam. And when she was finished with him, he'd wish he'd kept his distance

With her gun fisted on her hip, she yanked the door

open and glared up at him under the light of the single bulb illuminating the small front porch.

"What the hell are you doing here? Why aren't you with Pam?"

Justin drew his neck back, arched a brow and looked down at her like she was crazy.

"What the hell are you talking about?"

Delaine ignored his innocent, confused expression and ground her words into his face. "You. Slept. With. Pam! You bastard!"

"I slept with Pam? You've got to be kidding me!" he laughed.

Delaine quirked a brow, not seeing any humor in the situation. His laugh seemed genuine enough, but this was a man whose job was to be an expert at hiding who he really was. *As are you.* She ignored that little voice and, seeing no humor in the situation, scowled at him and his stupid laughter.

"Well, I'm not kidding! She answered your phone. You know, the one at your house. She said she was spending the night with you."

"And you believed her?"

"Well, she was there, wasn't she? What was I supposed to believe when she answered your phone at three in the morning?"

"But, Delaine …"

Her voice full of venom and pain, she bared her teeth and poked him in the middle of his chest with the barrel of her 9mm as she spoke. "And she sounded like she'd already been screwed good that night …"

"Delaine …"

"You lying, cheating son of a bitch! I should have known better than…"

Justin had enough. He was many things, but liar and cheat weren't on the list. He grabbed a very angry Delaine by the shoulders and shook her until her teeth snapped together. She flung away from him and headed into the cabin, intent on slamming the door in his face. He caught it with his foot just before it hit him in the nose, pushed the door open so hard it banged into the wall. He didn't care. He stomped into the cabin on her heels.

"Delaine, will you be quiet so I can tell you what's going on?"

"I don't want to be quiet! I want to tell you exactly what's on my mind, damn it!" She tossed her gun on the small rustic couch. "Better yet," she snarled and dropped into a fighting stance, "I think I'll just kick your ass!"

Justin's mouth dropped open. She was serious. Balanced on the balls of her feet, her strong arms were up, ready to strike. He watched the muscles in her thighs tighten and flex as she readied herself. His mind flew back to the last time he'd seen those thighs. They were wrapped around his waist, with her head thrown back while he'd sunk to the hilt. He shook his head to clear the distracting image.

All she wore was a little white camisole and a pair of silk bed shorts. To Justin, she'd never looked sexier or more pissed. Delaine's cinnamon skin was flushed with anger, and her chest rose and fell in agitation. The tops of her breasts peeked out from underneath her camisole. A light sheen of sweat made her body appear to glow in the dim lamplight. She was exquisite and fighting was the last thing he wanted to do with her. There was only one way to tame a woman who might be capable of beating you down.

Delaine watched him closely. Her brown eyes clashed with his smoldering blue ones and she knew he was calculating the distance between them. So he thought to take the upper hand, eh? Well, she was determined not to give it to him. She never used her fighting skills on people she knew, knowing she could seriously hurt them, but if he took one more step she was mad enough to lay him out. Damn, he stepped. And she let a right hook fly, ready to follow up with a roundhouse kick to the gut.

Eyes wide, her throat emitted a loud squeak when he

countered with a perfectly executed arm figure four move. As soon as she struck, he blocked her punch and grabbed her in the crook of her elbow with his free hand. She had a fraction of a second to wince as he bent her forearm up and back just before he stepped inside her defense and took her down to the floor. Hard.

The air whooshed from her lungs when her back hit the hard wood floor. The next thing she knew, Justin was lying at her side with his right shoulder on top of hers, and her right arm pinned underneath her. She couldn't move. Couldn't breathe.

Damn, that hurt. She instinctively tried to struggle. Justin put all his weight into the submission hold and Delaine went still. The slightest movement caused a funky pain to shoot up her shoulder and neck and then settle behind her eyes. Without releasing her from the hold, he slanted his mouth over hers and kissed the wind right out of her sails.

She had the ability to resist him for all of four seconds before she was lost in the taste of him as his tongue tormented hers. It seemed like forever since she'd enjoyed the way he explored her mouth, sucked and nibbled on her lips. He'd called her his cinnamon candy, and right now she certainly felt like it. He was eating her alive. Mmmm, she missed this. She whimpered when he pulled away from her lips.

He licked the corner of her mouth and rasped out, "Now will you listen?"

She nodded her head, eyes glazed over in a sensual stupor. Lord, the man sure could kiss. But he still hadn't let her out of the submission hold.

"Pam came to my house talking nonsense about how she wanted me. But nothing happened, Delaine. She was drunk out of her mind and it would have been wrong to send her home in that condition. Hell, she was so snockered, I'm still shocked she made it to my house."

"She said she spent the night with you."

"I wish I'd known you spoke to her, baby, because she spent the night with my couch. Before she passed out, I let her ramble on about how lonely she was and it turned out she didn't really want me. She just wants to be happy. I told her she needs to find her own man for that."

"That ho-humping bitch! Wait until I…"

"Delaine, she was so drunk, when she woke the next morning she didn't remember any of it. And I think the hangover was punishment enough."

Delaine looked deeply into his stormy blue eyes and saw nothing but truth. She reached out to her spirit guide. Sapa arose and padded to the forefront of her mind.

He tells the truth, Suta. Take what I offer, the lioness lent Delaine her keen sense of smell. Delaine lay still and inhaled deeply. No scent of Pam on him at all. The only female she smelled on him was herself.

"So she slept on the couch, eh?" she asked with a wry grin.

"Delaine, I slept in my bed alone with the door locked thinking about sinking my hard cock into nobody but you. Kind of like I'm thinking right now." Justin slowly released her from the submission hold and began to rub the feeling back into the arm he'd pinned underneath her.

He snickered, mocking himself. Now this was a shame. Here he was on the floor after a fight with a woman who could remove his head from his body, and his cock was hard as marble. It was pitiful, but he just couldn't help it. He slid his body on top of hers, held her arms above her head and pressed a very solid erection into her thigh. He began a slow, tempting grind.

"Oh goodness," she sighed, unable to resist the arousal he was stoking between them.

"Yeah, baby. Oh goodness is right," he whispered against her lips. Her face went up in flames and she blushed from her chest up to the roots of her dark, curly hair. Justin watched the heat move over her skin as his mind conjured an image of chocolate-covered cherries.

Damn, but she was delicious.

"Justin, I'm so sorry for the way I acted. About you being D.E.A. and about Pam. I feel really silly, especially since you didn't know what Pam had done. Hell, Pam didn't know what Pam had done." The last words were said on a gasp as one strong hand encircled her nipple through her silky camisole.

"I forgive you, baby." He lowered his head and tongued her sensitive nub through the silk.

"Sssss," she hissed, her neck and body arching into his, instinctively reaching for more of him. "God, that feels so good. Do you really forgive me?"

"Oh yeah. Want me to prove it?" his voice a soft, husky drawl just before he dipped his head and bit her on the sensitive spot on her neck.

* * * * *

Her arms curled around his neck as she arched her back, pulling him to her until her swelling breasts were pressed tightly to his chest. She opened expectantly when he lowered his head to take her in an open-mouthed kiss that stole her senses. He tasted of chocolate and man, and her tongue sought out every corner of his mouth as he kissed her. Sucking on that special spot on her neck, she threw her head back as the breath was pulled from her lungs in long, loud pants. Writhing and moaning at the indescribable sensation that always traveled through her whole upper body whenever he laved her there.

"What the hell?" she asked wildly when he untwined her arms, picked her up and deposited her on the thick rug in front of the fireplace, and rolled her over on her stomach. Her silk boxers slid down over her butt and off. Her camisole followed.

"You've been very bad, Delaine," he said much too softly.

"But you said you forgive me," she said breathlessly, trying to turn back again so she could wrap her legs around him and hold him close. Well, that was the plan anyway.

He obviously had other thoughts about the matter. "I do forgive you, but that doesn't mean you haven't earned a little punishment."

"Punish…ooooh!"

His hand landed with a loud smack on her bare ass. Oh damn, it felt good. The pleasure-pain sent a sensual twisting down through the nerves of her bottom and spread from her core outward.

He pulled her up to her knees and leaned forward. His breath tickled her ear, sending new shivers down the side of her neck. Pressing his huge cock into the crack of her ass, he asked in that sexy voice of his, "Do you like that, baby?"

Wiggling her ass to press closer to the hard, throbbing rod with an anxiousness that surprised her, she yelped when his hand landed on her ass again, sending a shockwave of need through her cunt.

"Oh shit! Yes—yes, I like it."

Delicious heat spread across her butt cheeks and settled just beneath her skin. She loved it, but she needed at least one more spank. Had to have it. Oh just one more. The urgency rivaled her need to be filled to bursting with his hard length. She'd never thought something so taboo as spanking could feel so good.

Her chest dropped to the rug and she hissed with pleasure, stretching her arms above her head to scratch and pull at the rug.

"Is there something you want, baby?" he purred against the sensitive skin on the back of her neck.

"Yes, I want it! I want…oh please."

His hands traveled from her warming bottom down to the crease at the back of her knees then around to the front of her thighs. Strong fingers pressed against the mound hiding her throbbing clit and pressed down firmly, while his other hand landed a final stinging smack on her right cheek. She came on the spot.

Unable to support her own quivering weight, she

collapsed on the rug, panting like she'd just run an eight-minute mile.

"You don't think you're getting away with that, do you? Baby, you've got some making up to do."

With her pussy still clenching and tightening, her lust was so easily rekindled. All it took was his strong hand pulling her back up to her knees and a deep plunge into her dripping channel.

A scream tore from her throat as he slid inside. The ridges and veins of his steel-hard cock stimulated every inch of her cunt. Every nerve ending fired, making her thighs quake and shiver with need. She'd just come but was already sobbing for him to give her more. Her nipples tingled as her breasts bobbed back and forth under his thrusts. His fingers unerringly squeezed and palmed her sensitive mounds without missing a single stroke. As he rode her hard from behind, not one inch of her skin was neglected as his hands roamed over her ass, her hips, her thighs.

The light sheen of sweat made the rough rasp of his palms feel decadent against her skin. His calluses raised gooseflesh followed by little licks of pleasure wherever they touched. She could feel her climax beginning in the heat centered in her body as her channel sought the eruption only he could give her.

Then he pulled out.

"Noooo!" She howled, looking over her shoulder as his huge body and massive cock poised just outside of her needy pussy.

"Convince me to give you more."

The look in his eye was one of pure male domination...and pain. She realized now how deeply she'd hurt him. After all, she would have felt the same way if he'd thought her low enough to sleep with his best friend. He'd forgiven her quickly enough, but his male ego needed a bit of stroking. Well, stroking was something she could definitely do.

She turned and sat up, taking him firmly in her hand and squeezing gently but firmly. He gasped at the contact, pushing his hips toward her questing fingers.

She didn't speak but used the pressure of her fingers to ease him forward, up off the floor and to the nearby couch.

She pushed him backward and he sat with his knees spread, looking up at her. His fingers wrapped around his cock and he pumped slowly. Her eyes glazed over with pure, unadulterated lust as her gaze shifted from the tempting motion of his cock up to his mouth where his tongue did a sensuous dance across his lips. She sank to her knees.

Without warning she circled the base of his magnificent staff with her fingers and dove over his cock, surrounding him with the warmth of her mouth. She took his feral yell as a good sign and moved her mouth up and down with relentless strokes. His hips moved in cadence with her strokes as his fingers tangled in her hair. She took him deeply and pulled back, allowing her tongue to swirl around the flared head on each up stroke. On the down stroke, she hummed long and loud.

When he began to shake she grasped the base tighter and jacked him harder.

"Del, stop! You're gonna make me cum!"

She stopped her torment long enough to say on a purr, "Well, that was the general idea." Then lowered her head to take him deeply. She never made it.

In a blink, Justin reached down, took her underneath her arms and lifted her onto his lap until she was on her knees facing him. She let out a gasp as he surged forward, seating himself in a single thrust.

"Sink down on my dick, baby! Oh, yeah!"

Wrapping her arms around his neck, she rose up and plunged back down, leaning forward to bite a stiff male nipple. There was nothing sweet or tender in her movements. It was all hard, rough and carnal. And she wanted nothing less. She tightened and released her canal around him with little pulses, bombarding him with sexual stimulus.

"Oh shit! Fuck me, baby! Give me that pussy, Del!"

Moving faster, she flexed her thigh muscles and slammed home, filling herself with his cock until she was sure she couldn't take anymore of him. A subtle shift of his hips brought her clit into constant contact with his rod and her body responded urgently, violently.

Palming her firm ass as she fucked him, she shuddered with anticipation when he reached back and found the spot where their bodies joined. She could feel him spreading her juices over and around her ass, teasing and tickling the tight, untried hole. The sensation was so intense it robbed her of any rational thought. All she knew was that she wanted him inside her in every conceivable way.

Reaching back to where he played with her hole, she singled out one of his long, thick fingers and placed it exactly where she wanted it.

He hesitated. She begged.

Her little tight hole was filled while his free hand rubbed the engorged length of her clit.

The cabin filled with primal, unrestrained shouts as they exploded together.

* * * * *

The cordless phone for Pam's direct line rang. She checked the caller id and smiled. It read Astin PharmaBio. It was Delaine. The woman worked too much, calling her from work on a Saturday. They hadn't talked in days and hoped to plan a get-together soon.

"Hey, girl, what's up?"

"Excuse me, is this Miss Pamela LeDoux?"

Ooops, Pam thought. Not Delaine, just some man calling from her office.

"Yes, this is Pam."

"I'm calling from Astin Pharmaceuticals. We're trying

to get in touch with Ms. Jeris. We know she's been ill, but we haven't been able to get her at home. We just wanted to check on her, see if she's all right."

"I'm sorry, but I can't help you. She's not here and I'm not scheduled to do her hair until next week."

"Well, sorry to bother you then. Thank you for your time, MissLeDoux. We'll try her at home again."

"No problem. Bye."

"Oh, wait, I have one more question. Unrelated to work, if that's all right?"

"Sure," Pam said, switching the phone to her other ear as she rinsed the shampoo out of a client's hair.

"A lady friend of mine just moved here and is looking for a beautician."

"This shop caters to women of color. No offense, but you don't sound like a person of color. What nationality is your friend?"

"She's black and very particular about her hair."

"Does she wear her hair natural or relaxed? We don't do relaxers, but I can recommend a good beautician if that's what she needs done."

"She wears her hair a lot like Ms. Jeris. And Ms. Jeris' hair always looks so nice and healthy."

Pam's mouth fell open. This guy must be gay or something to be this into a woman's hair. Especially if the woman wasn't sleeping with him, which she knew Delaine was not.

"How did Ms. Jeris find you?" the man asked. "Were you recommended to her?"

"Me? Oh, no," Pam laughed. "Delaine and I go way back. We're both from California, and we happen to be in North Carolina at the same time."

"Oh, how nice. So you're a very close friend, then?" the voice asked, with a friendly lilt. He sounded kind of English. Pam wondered if he was good looking. But it didn't really matter, because he still sounded gay. The oily quality of his voice flew right over her head.

"Yep. I'm pretty much the closest person to her on this side of the country."

"It's nice that she just moved here and has a close friend to spend time with. Well, thanks, Ms. LeDoux."

"No problem. Hey, what did you say your name was?"

"Uh, Schaller. Bobby Schaller. I'll have my friend call and make a private appointment."

"Sure, no problem. Bye." The call disconnected and Pam went on working. Lots of people promised to call for appointments. She didn't give it another thought.

*　*　*　*　*

Baker hung up the phone and sat back in his chair, stroking the hair of a dazed Sarah Ann kneeling between his legs under his desk. He thought about his chosen strategy to end Delaine's interference and chuckled before flipping open the cell phone to dial a number in Miami.

"Mr. Tapia, please. Tell him it's Baker."

After a few moments, a thickly accented voice came on the line.

"Tapia, here."

"Hello, Mr. Tapia. It's Baker. We've had an interruption in production, and I could use some assistance getting back on schedule."

"My time is valuable, Baker. Get to the point."

"I need you to send a few more of your associates up to Charlotte. Today."

"I already have twenty men planted in your town. If you can't handle this project, I won't send more. I'll just kill you."

"But that would be bad for business, both yours and mine. Look, I just need some assistance in getting the disrupter, as it were, to either cooperate or disappear."

"Fine. But the next time you call me, Baker, the news had better be good. Comprende?"

"Sí, comprende," Baker responded sharply before clicking the phone off. He hated the man. But he could deal with anything for the power it would bring him. After this project, Tapia would be on his own, and Baker would be king.

CHAPTER THIRTEEN

The weekend at Nantahala Gorge had been wonderful. Just her and Justin. No work. No interruptions. Just lots of fresh air, beautiful mountain trails, white rapids. And endless, hot, sweaty sex. Delaine couldn't believe how she'd whined when Justin burst her bubble by reminding her they needed to get back to Charlotte.

They packed and left the cabin late that night. Delaine transmitted the digital video of Baker's tests to both Derrick and Geri, then she and Justin talked by cell phone and developed a strategy as he followed her home from their haven in the Blue Ridge Mountains.

Justin opened Delaine's front door and held up his hand to keep her from stepping across the threshold. He signaled her to keep quiet as he pulled his gun out of the holster underneath his jacket and signaled silence. She nodded, retrieved her own sidearm and covered his back as he took the first step into her home.

Before Delaine could follow him, Sapa charged to the front of her conscience. The big cat's presence was so strong, it was almost overwhelming. Delaine took in a surprised gasp as the lioness' protective instincts surrounded her, strongly urging her not to enter the house.

But as always, Sapa couldn't overrule her. Any decision of what would be done was up to Delaine. But the lioness made her presence known. If Delaine needed her, she was there.

'Sapa, calm down and tell me what's going on here,' Delaine whispered along the psychic link.

Sapa's response confirmed Delaine's suspicions. Someone had been in her house. Nothing appeared to be missing, but the house had been carefully searched and everything put back in its proper place. Yes, someone had been here all right. Someone meticulous and very careful.

Justin left the lights off and set Delaine's weekend bag just inside the door. He signaled for her to take the upstairs while he searched the downstairs rooms. Delaine took off quietly up the stairs to search her bedroom. They met up in the kitchen and found a neatly folded piece of paper on the breakfast nook table. A note from Baker.

They looked at each other, silently communicating their rage. Both stiff and angry, they stalked to the phone together on the first ring. Pissed that someone would enter her private domain, she snatched the receiver off the hook and snarled a nasty hello. Her eyes went wide at the surprise of hearing Sarah Ann's shaky voice on the other end.

"H-Hi, Ms. Jeris."

"Sarah Ann? It's almost midnight. What are you doing calling me this late?"

"I want to help you. Can I come in?"

"Come in? What are you talking about?"

"I'm sitting in my car across the street from your house. I really need to talk to you. Can I come over? Please?"

"And why should I trust you?"

"Because I hate Brian Baker," Sarah Ann said on a choked sob.

"Well all-righty then. Come on over," Delaine said pleasantly.

Justin stood behind the door fuming as Delaine opened it for a clearly distraught Sarah Ann. He wasn't going to take the chance that Baker's confidante might show up armed, or worse, with Baker himself in tow. Delaine had argued against it, not wanting him to be seen at all. But Justin wasn't having it. He wanted Baker and anyone else to know that Delaine had a big, brawny, mad-as-hell ex-Jarhead at her back.

Delaine led Sarah Ann into the living room. Justin silently stalked behind them.

"Sarah Ann, would you like some tea?" Delaine asked, trying to distract the girl. Hands on hips, looking as calm as she was able, she asked what flavor she preferred.

"Jasmine Green Tea, if you have it," Sarah Ann said, smiling sheepishly. She looked up and her eyes bulged. Now that she was settled on the couch, there was no missing Justin as he stood on the steps that led into the sunken living room. She shrank into the cushions as the huge man glowered at her, the muscle in his jaw ticcing furiously. He stood not five feet away, his big muscular arms crossed over his even more muscular chest. His expression clearly read, "One wrong move and your ass is mine".

Sapa sent Delaine a mental picture of what Sarah Ann was feeling. Fear. Anger. Shame. All genuine. Delaine felt sorry for the woman. She'd been thrown into something she never wanted to be involved in. At least she had to guts to try to do something about it now.

"Sarah Ann, let me take your coat," Delaine said, trying to make her feel a bit more comfortable. Now it was Delaine's turn to gawk. Sarah Ann pushed her hood back and unzipped her coat. Delaine felt Sapa's ears prick forward. Sarah Ann's dark brown curly hair was now blonde!

Sarah Ann stilled at the intensity in Delaine's eyes as she stared at her hair. She lifted her fingers nervously, and tugged on an errant curl.

"I didn't want to be recognized, coming over here and all. I colored it just this morning."

Delaine continued to stare. The vision her spirit guide had shown her on that first night out with Justin came slamming back into her mind. The woman with the blonde hair was Sarah Ann! So what about the rest of the vision? Who was the woman tied up in a chair with a bag over her head?

The woman who seeks to help us is distraught. She is afraid of our mate.

Delaine silently nodded at Sapa's words and sweetly sent a menacing Justin to fix the tea. He could still see everything going on in the living room, but he still wasn't happy with the idea of leaving his woman alone with Sarah Ann. He gave Delaine his I'll-deal-with-you-later look and stalked off to the kitchen.

"So what's up, Sarah Ann? What can you tell us?"

Sarah Ann shivered with fear and glanced toward the kitchen. Her shoulders hunched forward as a stream of tears overflowed her eyes followed by a bout of rough, ragged sobs. Delaine gave her a moment to compose herself. Sarah Ann squared her shoulders, took a deep breath and pushed ahead.

"I hate what I've become because of Baker and his little experiments. He asked me to help him with research on a new product. After working late one evening he invited me for dinner at his place. We had one night of hot sex, and that's when he first slipped it to me. I'm a good scientist, Ms. Jeris. I had no idea he wanted to use me as a guinea pig."

Delaine felt such sadness at the pain in the woman's voice. Poor Sarah Ann bawled like a baby. Delaine sat down on the arm of the couch and discreetly motioned for Justin to quietly bring in the tea. He set the tray on the coffee table and turned to leave.

The corner of his mouth quirked up when he caught Delaine admiring his tight butt, but she didn't stop looking. She watched him stride back to the kitchen with the grace of a lion. With the exception of his blue eyes and fair skin, he reminded her of Sapa on the hunt. The set of his shoulders relayed his anger at Baker's audacity to enter her home. Delaine was glad they were on the same side. The man looked ready to kill.

"I swear, Ms. Jeris, I didn't know his secret project was a powerful synthetic aphrodisiac. The stuff is highly addictive and I didn't want the drug. When I told Baker I wanted him to find a way to counter the craving for it, he threatened to have me killed."

"Baker threatened to have you killed? Isn't that rather ballsy for him? He doesn't seem the type to want to get his hands dirty." Literally.

"He's got connections with some really bad people, Ms. Jeris."

"So how do you propose to help us?" Delaine asked, sipping her own cup of strong tea.

"I know Baker planned to leave you a note with a phone number on it. Have you called the number?" Sarah Ann asked, blowing delicately into her steaming cup.

"No, not yet."

"Good," she said, sitting the cup down gently on the coffee table. "The directions Baker left you are false. It's a trick. He knows you stole a tape from The Vault. He wants it back, but he's not stupid. He's got your friend, but ..."

"Whoa, whoa," Delaine stood to her feet, the tea all but forgotten. "What friend are you talking about?"

"Your beautician friend. His instructions, you haven't listened to them yet. You're supposed to meet him at Astin for an exchange, the videotape for your friend. But she won't be at the meeting place. She's being held at Baker's home on Lake Norman by some Cuban guys who came up from Miami."

"Why would he have people come up from another state?"

"Because that's who he's making the drug for. His

connections are Cuban mafia. Some big-time drug lord from down south. From Miami. He contracted Baker to create and make the drug. It's supposed to be the next big thing, the only truly synthetic and powerful aphrodisiac ever made. One that works on women in an explosive manner. If Baker fails to deliver, he'll lose his head and a few other choice body parts. He can't allow you to interrupt his plans, so he asked Tapia to send him some more muscle."

Delaine listened quietly as Sarah Ann confirmed what Justin had told her over the weekend about Baker and his mafia connection. A cold rage climbed up her spine, wrapping around her core with every word Sarah Ann spoke. Bastard. She couldn't wait to send him up.

"If you show up without the tape, he plans to have your friend injected with the drug. He's always tested it with a tablet to control the dosage better. With an injection, she'll have an instant reaction and overdose within half an hour. After his mafia thugs have fucked her silly."

"How do you know all this?"

"I let the creep think I was completely under his control. As long as I played the mindless bimbo, he didn't care if I was in the room while he conducted his business or not. I wasn't a risk."

"So what do you want out of this?"

"I want you to catch him, Ms. Jeris. Take him down."

"Done. Now tell us anything else we need to know."

* * * * *

It was three in the morning when Sarah Ann snuck out the backdoor and made her way around the side of Delaine's house to her car. What was it about this assignment and unexpected things happening at three in the morning?

Justin and Delaine called the number on Baker's note and listened to the pre-recorded message. He held Delaine's hand while adrenaline pumped their hearts up into their throats. The threats to Pam were explicit—deliver the tape or Pam was toast. But by the end of the message, both he and Delaine were shaking their heads in wonder. If the situation hadn't been so grave, they would have laughed out loud. Good ole Pam, loud and clear in the background, cussed her head off while telling Baker how she was going to kick his ass for making her miss work. They had to give her credit. The woman had a lot of guts. Now they had to keep her alive.

Justin lay face down on the carpet in front of the fireplace with a splitting headache. He was tense as a bowstring as the events of the night played over and over in his head. He groaned when he felt Delaine sit on top of his butt and begin to work the muscles of his back and shoulders.

"I can't believe I didn't figure this out before," she said quietly, kneading a particularly stubborn knot on his left scapula.

"Hmmm? What are you talking about?" he drawled sleepily. Delaine's fingers worked magic on his tired, aching back and he began to drift into a light doze.

"I still can't believe Sarah Ann was the blonde. And the bound woman in a chair with a bag over her head was Pam all along. Damn, I can't believe I missed it."

"Okay...so what are talking about?"

"Look, you're probably going to think I'm crazy but I got the information from someone who helps me with this kind of stuff. I was told about the blonde woman asking for help and the tied-up woman, but we weren't sure who they were." Delaine felt the honed muscles in Justin's back bunch and tense just before he turned over. She slid off his back and landed on her butt on the carpet beside him. He was all protective alpha now. Damn if she didn't like it.

"What kind of help? Better yet, who kind of help?"

Oh lord, the man was actually growling at her! Delaine was sure he didn't mean to sound so sexy, but it didn't change the fact that the deep rumbling made her skin ripple and her breath hitch in her throat. He was just so…everything! She instinctively felt the need to calm and reassure him.

"Justin, relax. It's not another man, if that's what you're thinking. It's a she. I have a spirit guide."

"A what?"

"It's a Native American thing."

"A Native American thing?" Cool, as long as it wasn't a man thing, it seemed he could handle it. He rolled to his stomach and Delaine climbed back on and continued her massage.

Delaine explained how Sapa had come to her when she was a little girl. At ten years old while out playing, she'd wandered to far from home and couldn't find her way back. She'd stared with wide eyes at all the cars whizzing by and almost peed her pants when an old streetcar rumbled past, shaking the ground underneath her small feet. On the verge of panic, she spotted a huge cathedral standing out from the rest of the crowded buildings and ran as fast as she could to its towering doors. She ducked inside and looked around frantically but didn't see anyone in the lobby or along any of the long candle-strewn aisles. Curled up in a dark corner, the tears gathered and fell in endless streams until she was all cried out. When she quieted, Delaine heard her grandmother's gentle voice in the far reaches of her mind.

'Meditate, child. Push away your fear and call on your spirit guide,' the voice said.

From as far back as she could remember, Delaine had spent every summer with her grandma on the Rosebud reservation up in South Dakota. Granny had taught her about God, called the Great Spirit or Wakantanka in the Lakota tongue. Whether Delaine was visiting the res or her granny had come to see her in California, she'd always taken the time to teach her little granddaughter of their ancestry, the importance of understanding their natural connection to the land, walking the old paths, and knowledge of natural and spiritual guides.

That day, a frightened and alone Delaine closed her eyes. She cleared her mind the way her grandma had taught her and called out to the Great Spirit with all her strength, heart and mind.

'Great Spirit? It's me, Delaine. Can you help me please? I'm lost and I want to go home. Granny said you would help me if I asked you to.'

That's when Sapa had come to her. The black female mountain lion calmed her with gentle strokes against her mind, sending concern and care through their newly forming bond. The lioness had been with her ever since, guiding her through dangers and sharing her spirit's wisdom through the years.

Justin's mouth hung open, but not because he thought she was crazy. He believed her. In fact, he not only believed her words, he was surprised to find he was somewhat jealous of Delaine and her guide. He'd never had such a close relationship with anyone, human or otherwise. And in his line of work, he'd expected to be alone until he died.

Since you love us, that will change. You will indeed be close to us.

Justin flew from his spot on the floor. "What the hell was that?" he yelled in surprise, dancing on the balls of his feet.

You are a worthy mate.

"Whoa!" Justin turned around in circles looking for who'd spoken.

Delaine rolled on her back, laughing while Justin looked at her like she'd grown two heads. She laughed harder, holding her stomach as the muscles clenched and spasmed with her giggles. When he turned a ghastly beet red in the face and looked ready to take on a gang of bad guys in a hand-to-hand fight, she calmed down long enough to explain.

"That was Sapa speaking into your mind, honey."

"Sapa?" he gasped, looking around like he expected to see a big black feline stalking around Delaine's living room. Delaine felt Sapa send his mind a calming push. He settled enough to finally ask, "How did she do that? And what did she mean?"

"She said that since you love us…wait," Delaine's eyes went wide on a pause. "You love me, Justin?" After the way she'd kicked him to the curb? The way she'd acted about his job when she hadn't even considered telling him about hers? She cared for him deeply, no doubt about that. But could he really?

Justin joined her on the floor and gathered her into his arms until they were face to face, nose to nose.

"I do love you, Delaine Jeris. I love you more than anything or anyone."

Delaine tried to check the tears gathering behind her eyes. Since they wouldn't listen she closed her eyes and ducked her head beneath his chin as her heart slammed in her chest. He loved her? Already? And after the way she'd treated him?

"B-But we haven't known each other that long," she whispered disbelievingly.

"Baby, I don't know how, but I do know why. You're beautiful, Delaine, inside and out. You're strong, but vulnerable. You're honest, caring. I can't explain how I feel what I feel, but just know that I do, with all my heart, love you, baby. You're my Lakota queen, my dark-eyed love. From the top of your kinky head to the soles of your feet, I love you."

She bawled earnestly now as he stroked her hair, and Justin could have sworn he felt her happiness, her amazement, swirling in his head just out of reach. His large hand stilled, his hand in mid-stroke down Delaine's back. He could swear he heard…purring? Sultry, deep purring.

"It's Sapa, honey. I hear her too," Delaine said, snuggling closer against his chest.

"So what does it mean?"

"It means she accepts you. You love me, so Sapa shares herself with you."

"Has, uh, has this ever happened before? You two ladies, giving yourselves to one lucky man?" For some reason he had to know if she'd felt this close to anyone else, even her ex-husband. He broke out in a broad grin at her response.

"No, she's never, I mean we've never done this before. And there's something else I've never done," she crooned, raising her head from his chest and repositioning her body to straddle him. With trembling fingers, she stroked his cheek while her deep brown eyes locked with his. He tilted his head, wondering at her soft yet serious expression. Then two simple but powerful words tumbled from her mouth.

"My name," she whispered.

He said nothing, but the bottom of his stomach roiled as he regarded her. She couldn't possibly be doing what he thought she was doing, could she? She opened her mouth to speak again and his head started throbbing. Well, no wonder—he'd stopped breathing.

"I-I uh." She snapped her mouth closed, looked down at a spot on his shirt somewhere around his pecs and took a deep breath. When she raised her lashes, he saw everything she wanted to say right there on her beautiful face. The love and care she felt for him was all visible, but would she say the words? He started to tell her that it was okay, that she didn't have to say or reveal anything she didn't want to. Before he could get the words out, their world changed forever.

"Justin, I love you too. And my name is Alesia. Alesia Younglion. The only people in the world who know are my children, my boss. And you."

Justin was sure his heart had never been so full of emotion in his life. This woman floored him, and he was simply undone. A lone tear made a path down his cheek and Delaine, uh, Alesia, gently kissed it away. After a moment, the bands around his chest loosened and he pulled her to him for a tight hug and a quick kiss before easing her back a bit to take in her lovely face.

"How do you say it?" When she tilted her head in confusion, he said, "In your grandmother's tongue. Your name, how do you say it?"

"Younglion? Igmutanka Ojilaka."

"Mmm," he groaned, leaning forward to swipe his tongue across her full bottom lip. "Sounds much sexier than Cooley." Her giggle warmed his insides.

"Damn, you and Ms. Sapa sure know how to sweep a guy off his feet." His voice dropped to a husky drawl, full of emotion and just a hint of smart-ass-ism.

"Oh shut up and kiss me already," Delaine laughed up into his face. He brought his lips down in a hard, demanding kiss as strong hands dropped to the curve of her ass and slipped underneath to gently finger her jean-covered core. Chuckling into her mouth when she squirmed, he proved that now it was her turn to purr.

* * * * *

Their plans were finalized after a last phone call to Derrick and Geri. Too tired to do anything but snore, they made it to bed just before sunup. The instructions on the tape told Delaine to meet Baker at midnight, so they slept in until Justin woke Delaine with tender kisses across the sensitive spot on her neck.

Delaine had spent the afternoon teaching Justin how to call Sapa and recognize the lioness' push against his mind. It was eleven forty-five, and Delaine was in the elevator headed down to The Vault. She summoned Sapa into her corporeal form and sent her ahead to scout. The big cat sent clear images of who was waiting below to both her and Justin.

Delaine stepped out of the elevator and was met by two armed men she'd never seen in the Astin facility before. She knew Baker and ten more thugs waited in and around the lab she'd snagged the samples and videotape from…Sapa's reconnaissance also confirmed Sarah Ann's tip—Pam was nowhere in the building.

She was taken to Baker in the back room. Her two escorts had kept their hands to themselves until now. Suddenly her elbows were yanked painfully behind her back. She instinctively schooled her features into a bored mask as a sharp pain lanced from the joint up through her shoulder blades. Determined to convince the idiots she was powerless, she bided her time with a deep, calm intake of breath and forced herself not to pull away from the men and thrash them into the ground.

Baker turned his steely-eyed gaze on her and smiled nastily. Sapa roared in her head, wanting Delaine to take him down fast. The lioness quieted after Delaine reminded her Justin and the backup they'd called in needed a few more minutes to get into position. Baker's cultured voice interrupted her conversation with her spirit guide.

He stepped much too close and skimmed the backs of his fingers along the underside of her breasts. Delaine ignored him and painted on her who-gives-a-damn face. Her stomach heaved and her skin crawled, but Baker would never have the satisfaction of knowing she was ready to hurl her dinner. He spoke softly, like a gentle lover.

"Where's the tape, Jeris?"

"I didn't bring it, asshole, but it's someplace safe. I didn't trust you to have Pam here. Since I don't see her in this room, I guess I was right." She focused her thoughts and asked Sapa to send Justin a mental picture of what was going on.

"Well, that's too bad for your friend, isn't it?" Baker scoffed. He flipped open his phone and pushed the speed dial. After a few seconds he hung up, his brow furrowed. But he quickly recovered, replacing his frown with a carefree grin.

"So tell me, Ms. Jeris. Who exactly are you? Who do you work for?"

Geesh, what a stupid question, Delaine thought as she looked at him like he was as dumb as a bucket of raisins. She didn't bother to answer. Baker knew damned well who she was. He'd known since the day she arrived.

"You know," Baker drawled, "I don't like your nonchalance. You're in a good bit of trouble, young lady, yet you don't seem concerned." The last word was said as he stepped back and backhanded her smartly across the face. Again Delaine reined in her temper even as her neck snapped sideways. Her calmness only seemed to make Baker madder. Good.

Her lip quirked up into a condescending smile. Bastard. Just wait until she was free. She was going to kick his ass. Blood pooled into her mouth from the small cut he'd opened up at the corner of her mouth. She gathered a nice wad of it and spit it directly into Baker's face.

The wad landed on his right cheek, and he recoiled as if a snake had bitten him, as if her spit was the vilest thing on the planet. He quickly retrieved a sparkling white handkerchief from his lab coat pocket, wiped his face and threw the soiled piece of cloth in the trash bin near his feet. Then he smiled the most chilling, unsettling show of teeth Delaine had ever been on the receiving end of.

"You know, my lovely Ms. Jeris, I've heard that sliding between the legs of a black woman is a life-changing experience. I've never had the pleasure. Until now."

"Please," Delaine spat. "You think I'd give you some of this? You're crazier than I thought."

"No, not crazy. Empowered. And in just a few minutes, you'll be begging me to fuck you."

Delaine laughed outright. Not a cute little chuckle. No, this was an all-out, full belly laugh. He had no idea who he was fooling with. But he'd sure as hell find out, and soon. All he had to do now was make his biggest and final mistake. She didn't have long to wait.

Delaine stoically watched Baker as he walked over to a locked cabinet. He pulled out a large banker's box full of packages that looked like plastic bricks full of little pink candies. He ripped one open and retrieved a single pink tablet before turning his malevolent glare on her.

Baker approached with the tablet balanced on the end of his finger, just as he'd done to the woman on the digital video. But Delaine wasn't that woman. As soon as he stood in front of her, he commanded her to open her mouth.

Then all hell broke loose.

* * * * *

Justin and a team of D.E.A. S.W.A.T. crept through the seldom-used tunnels he and Delaine had escaped through before. Justin gritted his teeth as the images of what Delaine was facing streamed into his mind. It practically killed him to allow his woman to face their enemy alone. Hell, he was still trying to figure out how she'd talked him into this cockamamie plan. Slowly getting used to a presence in his head, he was only a bit startled when Sapa spoke into his thoughts.

In time you will become less surprised at the persuasiveness of your mate, Akicita Justin.

Delaine had explained to him earlier that the great lioness had nicknamed him, Akicita, "warrior" in the Lakota tongue. He didn't feel like much of a warrior right now, but knowing Sapa had dealt with Delaine's stubbornness since childhood made him feel at least a bit less inept.

Dealt with her stubbornness? As our Suta would say, you have no idea.

Justin snorted quietly. If a spirit couldn't rein her in, then he must not be such a bad mate after all. Sapa's calm assurance, lots of deep breathing and fantasizing about what he was going to do to Baker kept him from bursting into the room. His grip tightened on the handle of his gun when Baker backhanded Delaine across the face, but he kept still, hiding in the closet without a sound. When Baker had the drug in front of Delaine's face, on his signal, he and his team burst through the closet doors and filled the room.

* * * * *

One of the men holding her released her arms and ran for the door. The idiot opened the door and ran right into the fists of several armed law enforcement officers. S.W.A.T.! Yeah, she'd know them anywhere. She inwardly winced at the sickening sound of fists sinking into flesh, and the thug was quickly down. His friend, who appeared to be a little smarter, grabbed her by her arm again, but this time she had a hand free.

Her technique was clean and quick. With her free hand she backhanded her captor across the bridge of his nose with a closed fist. His head snapped back on his neck like a rubber band pulled too tight. She stepped back and gave him a clean kick to the ribs and he went down like a sack of potatoes tossed off the back of a truck.

Delaine felt Sapa pushing at her mind with urgency. What was her spirit guide doing? The lioness was supposed to be looking out for Justin. Urgency rushed through the bond and Delaine turned to find herself facing a very angry, charging Baker.

"Noooooo! I won't let you ruin me!" Baker screamed, running toward Delaine brandishing a very heavy-looking, stainless steel lab tool.

Delaine recognized a mad scientist when she saw one. If he was going down, he was determined to take somebody with him. And right now, she appeared to be a perfect candidate. Unarmed, he was on her so quickly she only had time for a single thought.

"Sapa! Help!" Delaine yelled out loud.

Take what I offer, Suta.

Delaine felt her body fill with the strength of the lioness. Her skin tingled with untapped power as she saw Baker through the eyes of her spirit guide. No longer the big bad villain. He was now prey.

Time slowed. Even Baker appeared to move in slow

motion as he charged her with his makeshift weapon in one hand and the fingers of his free hand tensed and curled like claws. The second his clammy hands wrapped around her neck, she slipped her hands up between his outstretched arms, took a single step in and swept his legs from under him. As he was falling backward, she checked with her hip and he went flying over her back. On his way down to the floor, she slammed his head into the concrete. But the rest of his body continued to fly. In the end, there was an unmistakable crunch when his chest met his face. His neck and every vertebra down to the middle of his back snapped like dry dead twigs.

Sapa roared in her head as Delaine growled low in her throat, breathing heavily. The surge of strength and power slowly subsided as the lioness retreated from the forefront of her mind. Delaine hated taking a life. She'd been raised to always respect life, no matter how rotten or corrupt. She was grateful when Sapa sent peace and pride through the bond. The spirit of the lioness would always fight to protect her loved ones. She was the ultimate hunter and refused to be ashamed of defending those in her care.

Delaine looked down at Baker, his wide green eyes unseeing, and his pale face permanently etched with stunned disbelief. Sapa flashed images to her of what was happening all over the building. Baker's boys had been rounded up, none escaped. The premises were being searched for more evidence, though the box full of pink tablets in the still unlocked cabinet was more than enough.

Then Justin was at her side, pulling her into a warm embrace before hauling her toward the door.

"Justin, wait. We've got to do a mop-up here."

"Not today, baby. Derrick's already called in another team to do it. We've got to get to the hospital."

"Hospital? Why?"

"When our boys burst into Baker's house at Lake Norman, Pam was in the middle of an almost successful escape. One of the bad guys shot her, baby."

"What!?"

"I said, Pam's been shot. Let's go."

* * * * *

Delaine stepped into the sparsely furnished hospital room. The orange roses in her hand offered the only relief against the sterile white furniture, walls and curtains. She set the glass vase of flowers on the nightstand and Pam's eyes fluttered open.

"Hey, girl. How are you feeling?" Delaine asked quietly, a slight smile across her lips.

"Like somebody spent the night kicking my ass."

"Well, I'd like to kick your ass too, ya know."

Pam smiled weakly, her words a bit slurred by the wonderful morphine drip on her IV. "I know, and I don't blame you, Del. And I'm so sorry. I was so drunk I didn't realize what I'd done until later the next evening. After lots of coffee and lots of sleep. Justin didn't have anything to do with it. It was all me, girl. But we never slept together. As a matter of fact, he practically ran from me while singing your praises, even though you were mad at him."

Delaine chuckled and said, "I know, Pam, but I wasn't talking about that. I was talking about you trying to get away from several armed men, you idiot." She reached out and gently touched her friend's hand to take the sting out of her words.

"What can I say, Delaine. I wasn't thinking, I just reacted. I couldn't let that bastard use me to blackmail you. You're my girl."

Delaine was touched. She felt so special. She'd never thought to have a man like Justin, nor reunite with an honest, caring friend like Pam. Her chest clogged with emotion and she almost missed the faint scent of Justin's cologne amidst the non-smells of the hospital room. He touched her about the waist and hugged her lightly from behind. She turned slowly, her eyes close to spilling over.

"Hi, baby," he crooned, nuzzling her ear. "How are you holding up, sweetheart?"

"I'm all right, I guess." In fact, she'd refused to allow the events of last night to sink in yet. She'd been on plenty of dangerous missions, but not once had she ever been compromised. And she'd never been in love with the person watching her back. If Justin hadn't insisted on covering her, she could have easily been taken out. If even one part of their plan had gone wrong, her children could have been left without a mom. Or she could have lost this wonderful man who'd stood by her side because he cared enough to put himself in danger, even risk his career, to see her safe. It was a humbling realization.

"Hey, Pam," Justin stepped away from Delaine and moved around the side of Pam's hospital bed. He placed a chaste kiss on her forehead and set a colorful get-well card on her little tray stand.

"Hey, Jus. I apologized to Delaine for that misunderstanding at your house that night. Now I need to apologize to you."

Justin returned to Delaine's side and draped his arm over her shoulder. He looked down at her with a lopsided, boyish grin and said, "It's all right, Pam. We're all good."

The door slid silently open and a short, dark-haired woman called cheerfully from the door. "Hello there, I'm Dr. Lampshire." She removed a clipboard from the slot, checked over the chart and greeted Pam as she entered the room.

"How are you, Pamela?" she asked, adjusting the IV drip. At Pam's grumbled "just fine, thanks", she continued in a friendly tone. "The surgery went well, and there is no sign of infection. If you continue to improve, you can go home in a couple of days. Is there anyone in your family available to take care of you for a few days after you're released? If not, I'll give the okay for you to stay past the required amount of time."

Pam winced as the doctor gently probed the dressing over the gunshot wound high on the left side of her chest.

"Doctor, Pam recently moved here and doesn't have

any family. We go way back. She can come stay with me."

Delaine looked up at Justin and found his eyes on her. He winked and said, "Pam, you can come stay with us." Her brows rose, but she didn't gainsay him.

"Us?" Pam wondered aloud. Her eyes widened as much as they were able considering the amount of pain medicine she was enjoying.

"Yes, us. I'm not letting this woman out of my sight, and whether she's at my house, or I'm at hers, she's stuck with me. And you're stuck with the both of us. Or," he added dryly, "you can stay here and enjoy an endless supply of Jell-O."

Pam grimaced and informed the doctor she would indeed be going home with Delaine and Justin.

ABOUT THE AUTHOR

TJ is an award-winning author of several romance genres, including paranormal, fantasy, sci-fi and urban fantasy romance. Writing like a madman, TJ hasn't lost steam. Her mind? Yep, that's gone, but steam there is a-plenty. A true Taurus, TJ isn't slowing down and she's definitely too stubborn to stop when she sees the fence!

No matter the genre TJ is penning, her favorite thing to do is build worlds. To take you somewhere extraordinary. To transport you to a place where you can close your eyes and slip into your fantasy...

ALSO BY AUTHOR TJ MICHAELS

Carinian's Seeker, Vampire Council of Ethics Book One
Serati's Flame, Vampire Council of Ethics Book Two
Hatsept Heat, Vampire Council of Ethics Book Three
Seeker's Solace, Vampire Council of Ethics Book Four
Silk Road, Seals of Destiny
Spirit of the Pryde, A Pryde Ranch Shifter Story
Niah's Pride, A Pryde Ranch Shifter Story
Jaguar's Rule
Forever December
Egyptian Voyage
On the Prowl
Entwined Hearts
Shards of Ecstasy
Caramel Kisses
Death and Roses
Mastered: Ten Tales of Sensual Surrender
Juicy, A Twilight Teahouse Tale

Turn the page for a preview of TJ Michael's Holiday
paranormal romance novella "Forever December"

FOREVER DECEMBER

Michael had never before seen Melaniece's mouth fall open as her skin went pale. It would have been comical if it hadn't been so important for her to be happy to see him. He strode into the living room in his socks. Though his steps were deliberately slow and easy, he was so eager to wrap the woman in his arms that it still felt like he was practically running.

"Michael? What the hell are you doing here?" Melaniece gasped, still sprawled on the floor in front of the fireplace. Damn she looked sexy. It was just like he'd imagined in his dreams—her lying in front of the fireplace waiting for him to ravish her lush, beautiful body.

Suddenly she sprang up from the floor with a wild-eyed expression like she'd been caught with her hand in the cookie jar. And she didn't look happy to be caught, at least not by him. But that was just too bad. He'd come all this way only for her, and he'd be damned if he wasn't going to have her.

"Hi, Mel," he deliberately crooned, knowing how much she loved his "deep" voice. "Aren't you glad to see me, babe?" he asked stretching out his arms to her. Arms that

156

had become well acquainted with holding her during her last trip home. And there was nothing like cuddling with Melaniece Matthews. But this time, there was no need to leave it at cuddling. No need for her to assure him he was more than ordinary in spite of his crumbled marriage. Self-confidence restored, he was all man standing in her house with outstretched arms. Hell, screw a cuddle, she looked so deliciously surprised standing there in her skintight tee and comfy sweats, her hair all over her head, nervously nibbling on her bottom lip. He wanted to strip her bare with a smile, right here, right now.

Her tongue seemed stuck to the roof of her mouth. But Michael, being his old self once again, didn't wait for her to acclimate. Instead he pulled her into his arms and wrapped them around her until his nostrils were full of the scent of delicious, mouthwatering woman. And it was absolutely decadent.

"Mmmm, it feels so good to hold you again, Mel. Merry Christmas, beautiful."